Nightmares & Lullabies

Also by Ronald McGuire

Beyond Tomorrow's Sun
Beyond the Rivers of Time
Pax Liminalis

Nightmares

&

Lullabies

Collected Stories

Ronald McGuire

Beach Book Press

Published by Beach Book Press, Norwell, MA
First Edition, 2024

10 9 8 7 6 5 4 3 2

Library of Congress Control Number: 2024918490

Paperback ISBN: 978-1-965621-02-8

Ebook ISBN: 978-1-965621-03-5

This collection is dedicated to independent publishers, who gave many of these stories their first home. And to writers everywhere whose stories have yet to be heard.

"We write to taste life twice, in the moment and in retrospect."
–Anaïs Nin

Previously Published

Early Summer, *The Dillydoun Review*
Timing the Turn, *Screen Door Review*
Shoes, *Drunk Monkeys*
Fitting In, *The Dead Mule School of Southern Literature*
Also, Honorable Mention, Tom Howard/ John H. Reid Fiction & Essay Contest Reprinted by *Winning Writers*
Farewell, Hollywood, *Flash Fiction Magazine* (as "What Are They Eating on Mars These Days?")
Dust and Memories, *Cinnabar Moth Literary Collections*
Ghosts of Winter, *Top 10, Writer's Digest Short-Short Story Contest*
The Not-Zombies Apocalypse, *Cinnabar Moth Literary Collections*
A Time to Dance, HauntedMTL "Queer as Hell" Anthology (as "Transmigration of a Serial Killer")
Lullby, *Flash Fiction Magazine*

Early Summer

I looked once, then again after a pause, and like each time before, he was just then approaching down the sidewalk. I spin my head back to my book as if hiding my shame from some unknown witness. Yes, I was ashamed to want him, to see him even, walking by our little stoop.

Not ashamed to see him I suppose, but to be seen looking. My eyes couldn't possibly hide my heart.

His schedule had become irregular and tortuous, his timing twisting me into knots as I tried to time my reading to his arrival. I could never know, and often spent extra hours on the hard stone steps rising up to my family's brownstone, trying to focus and not focus on whatever book I had that day.

It was strange to be so alone and feel so encumbered by those around me all at once, so public felt my presence.

Yet there I sat, day after day, well-worn pages of my paperback in hand, like a bumblebee waiting for the first sign of spring, as if that happened every day.

He was not entirely handsome, yet somehow appealed to my most entrenched desires. Not terribly tall, but tall enough. Not slender or slight, but built just so, somewhere between beautiful and frightening. Athletic to be sure, but a bit grotesque with his wrestler's ears.

I didn't mind that extra flesh aside his skull. It matched all the other thick and meaty parts and pieces I could see as he sauntered down the sidewalk towards me.

That's how I imagined it, him walking to me, not by me. In my mind he saw me as I saw him. Not in the same way, as a thing of beauty and majesty to witness and behold. Not that, given my condition. No, as I saw him in the moment - I witnessed his movement and, in that experience, he witnessed my stillness.

One day he did see me.

His eyes were darker than I expected when they landed on mine for the first time. I meant to take note of this when it happened, not after, but he shattered my inner life with his smile.

He stopped, there on the walk, right at my feet, where I sat atop the rampart of my family fortress.

Perhaps I only imagined the rays of sunlight splashing around his shoulders, reflecting black sheen off his glossy cropped hair. If I did, it was a sweet dream of a moment. If I did not, then it was a glorious thing to know.

He looked up and smiled, his slight olive skin flowing effortlessly into his close-cropped cut, all that tussle left atop his head, like brambles along the edge of a freshly topped road.

Then he spoke, his voice flowing into me like the air I'd stopped breathing when he stopped walking.

"Hi," he said, as if he planned it, "you're Randy, Tommy's little brother, right?"

I'd spent innumerable hours imagining our first conversation, playing out in my mind how it might happen, how I would impress and enthrall him with my genius, my erudite wit.

When the time came, all I could say was "Yeah, he's my brother. He's a jerk."

I cringed at my utter failure, knew all my dreams had been ruined, felt my soul caving into nothing, blood rushed to my face and I was about to bolt into the refuge of our castle and was stopped cold when he said, "Yep, that's Tommy alright," a smile filled with knowing writ large across his face.

"So," he went on, "watch ya doin'?"

I held up my book, Moby Dick, for him to see, incapable of speech.

"Oh, yeah, guess I shoulda known, book in ya hand an all," and now he was blushing.

In that moment, everything changed, a little. The universe shifted to one direction just a fraction of an inch and I knew he was just like me. Nervous and hopeful and wanting, all alone.

"Where ya goin'," I asked, as if I didn't know.

"I'm goin' for a swim, down at L Street, wanna come with?"

"What," I say to give my heart a chance to slow, "you got a membership down there?"

"Well yeah, my pops does, I wouldn't be goin' if I didn't," he tells me and I feel my face burn again.

"Cm'on," he says, "I get to bring a pal anytime, whatdya say?"

Faced with the realization of a dream come true, I'm frozen into inaction born of one simple truth.

"I don't have no suit," I say, and it's the truth.

"You don't need one down L Street, it's all fellas, everybody goes skinny," he says with a smile that could win lotteries.

I set free my desire so it could crush my fear and say, projecting a casual air with as much success as someone caught stealing, "Okay, sure."

"Let's go then buddy, the free sodas ain't gonna last long so we gotta get a move on."

He sweeps one arm out southward toward the water and I stand, leaving my book to flutter its lost pages in the breeze on the stoop. I step down and rejoice when I find we're almost the same height, me just a tad shorter.

He throws his arm across my shoulders bringing heaven down upon me and we walk south together as he tells me all about the L Street Swimming club and how we'll have so much fun and the sodas are free and I am already there before we reach the next block.

It's early summer, and my life has just begun.

Timing the Turn

The locker room was a place I never understood. But I never sought out organized sports until I started high school. I joined the swim team because I liked the water. I was good at swimming, even better at attracting the attention of some of the older boys after practice. I was tall for my age. I didn't understand their attention until later, until I'd learned the truth about the world. But I knew who I was, even then.

One finally broke the silent barrier of looks and moves and eyes wandering. The space came so naturally to him, but not me. He asked me, standing there naked, all seventeen years of him, if I'd swum on a team before.

"No," I said, and used my towel to hide.

"You're good," he said, hiding nothing, "but your turn is sloppy, your timing sucks."

"How do I..."

"Coach doesn't give a shit about freshman. If you wanna learn, I can teach you."

"I don't..."

"Do you wanna fix that flop or not?"

I had to look at something. The locker felt like cowardice, the floor felt like shame, the ceiling never occurred to me, so I settled on his eyes. "Yeah, I'm new..."

"No shit Sherlock," he said. "Can you stick around?"

"No...my mom is waiting..."

"Too bad, maybe next time."

He turned, twisting the world around him, tossing me away and behind.

There was never a next time. I wondered for years about his motives. The time came when I imagined his intentions, dreamt of them, and wished I'd stayed there and learned to time the turn. Sophomore year I played football.

I lost track of him that year and tried to purge his presence from my thoughts, even as his memory lingered against my will. I was a freshman in college when I saw him again, in another locker room. I was approaching nineteen. A lot had changed. He recognized me as I did him. There was more of him to see, a statuesque structure of muscle built on the foundation of his youthful swimmer's build, beautiful cliché in bronze.

"Well, look at you, all grown up."

I reveled in his recognition.

"You too," I said, looking down from the height attained in a spectacular burst of growth my junior year. For sport I looked him over, returning the favor of years ago. I wasn't shy anymore.

"You been workin' out here all year?" he asked.

"No, since the season ended, when it rains. Closer to my dorm." I didn't care what he was about to ask me.

"So, you wanna..."

"Yes."

"OK," he laughed, "meet me out front." He started back toward his clothes, then stopped.

"You drink beer?"

"No, how about some coffee," I said.

"Sure, ok, coffee it is," he tossed back and continued walking.

He took his time taking his leave and I took full advantage.

I showered and dressed in a hurry, part of me expecting not to see him again. He was there, waiting beneath the portico, leaning against a concrete column in jeans and a crimson jacket, a modern-day James Dean.

"Okay to walk?" he asked.

"Sure," I said, "the rain's not too bad."

Somewhere between there and the coffee shop, halfway between heaven and earth, as our conversation built a bridge across time, he slipped his hand into mine as easy as a letter into a box, enough pressure for me to know he meant it.

"Have you been waiting for me?" I asked.

He laughed and gave a squeeze that found its way up my arm, swirled around my chest, then landed in my brain, reassuring me the laughter wasn't cruel.

"No," he said, "well, maybe. I've been waiting for someone. Now here you are."

"How did you know, back then?"

"High school? Are you kidding? I didn't know shit. I knew I liked you, but I couldn't say why. Mostly I was scared. Part of me thought you didn't like me because I'm black."

"You're more brown than black," I said, quoting a movie.

"And you're more pink than white," he said, catching the reference like an outfielder catches a pop fly.

I thought about what might have been, had I been a little older. I never saw him as scared, but in retrospect it made sense.

"What about you?" he asked.

"I think I'm what they call a late bloomer," I said.

"Well, you've definitely bloomed, if that's the analogy you want to use," he said.

Our laughter echoed across the brick wall and pathway, collected by the falling rain shushing through the branches watching over us.

We reached a turn that would take us from the secluded

pathway, through a colonnade, then into the open quad. I pulled him to a stop.

"I think you have been waiting for me," I said.

"What makes you…?"

"Because I've been waiting for me too," I said, "it makes sense."

"You have to explain that one."

"Even if we didn't understand then, we both knew what we wanted. I just had to catch up, and maybe you had to slow down. Like you said, here we are."

He leaned in to kiss me, our first kiss, my first kiss. It shook my core and left me gasping for air.

"I caught you," I said, my words forming clouds above us.

We stepped into the open and his hand fell from mine as a stone falls from a ledge. The windows of the quad stared down, innumerable eyes behind their darkness. Our separation a silent acknowledgement that we weren't as fearless as we thought, disquiet measurable in the space between us.

We covered a lifetime in a hundred paces, then left the monoliths of higher education behind, his hand again finding mine. We would not live that way forever. We learned to live our lives at our own deliberate pace, giving the world time to catch up to where we'd arrived, hand in hand no matter who was watching.

Shoes

If I ask about your shoes, there's a reason. I was sitting in the waiting room - I'd driven a long way to see this one particular doctor - and I knew I had a long wait. There was an elderly gentleman sitting alone when I got there. I checked in, then sat down near him. I was filling out a stack of forms - I was a new patient and I had to tell them my life story. Do they think I remember the date I had my tonsils out? Let's skip that line. I sit down, start filling in lines that are too small for my handwriting, and this elderly gentleman compliments my shoes.

I'm deliberate about my shoes. I have shoes for every occasion. As a bonus, my shoes last a long time. I have some I've never worn. I'm convinced one day I'll be in a forest with an axe and those steel-toed shin-high American-made Red Wing boots will say, "I told you so."

"Those are nice shoes you have. One must have good shoes, and those you have are very nice."

He says this with a German accent. I know this because I'd spent the summer in Germany, and, yes, I speak German.

Everybody in Germany wanted to speak English. Everybody except the people protesting against the US military. What did they expect? We send plane-loads of 18 and 19 year-old kids over there and you think they're all gonna behave? No way.

That didn't have anything to do with me. I was there with my backpack kicking around while the Berlin wall was being broken down into a billion little pieces. I got bored after a while, so I hopped a train to Greece while I waited for the guy I met in Italy to meet me in Belgium to go to a concert. I thanked God, and my parents, every day I was there for the Unlimited Eurail Pass.

I speak enough German that I knew his accent was German.

I thanked him in German, which is easy, and you would have thought I handed this man a bucket of gold coins. He was really happy. Which, to be honest, made me happy.

Since we didn't have anything else to do, we talked about shoes. In German. Well, not entirely in German. My vokabular was pretty good, but it wasn't that good.

He believed shoes were important, that you could learn a lot about someone from their shoes, and even more from how they felt about their shoes.

Maybe it sounds weird or crazy, but the alternative was to sit there in silence and wait to get called back to see the Doc. Why not have a conversation in German about shoes instead?

I don't remember every word, but we kept at it until his grandson sat down next to him.

This is when things got interesting.

His grandson, a handsome dark-haired twenty-something with a lovely smile and a beautiful soft baritone voice, sat down after finishing up at the check-out counter. Is that what it's called? I don't know, the place in the office where you pay and set your next appointment, if you need one.

The handsome grandson sits down and listens to us talk in German then gives me this big perfect-white-toothy smile before he introduces himself. For the barest of seconds I thought about hitting on him, then I checked myself.

Grandson wore a ring.

I asked grandson if he spoke German too, and he laughed and said, "No way, my grandmother forbid it. My dad doesn't speak German either."

Oh. That's curious. What's up with that?

Grandad sees the look on my face and starts to explain.

He told me how he fled Germany as a young boy, when the Nazis took over. He escaped, his future wife escaped, and both of them lost their entire families to the concentration camps.

They each, separately, made it to England, with lots of help along the way, especially in France. Their paths didn't cross until they were placed with two different families on the same street in London. Then they had to get out of London because the verdammt Nazis were bombing the hell out of the place.

They met, they fell in love, they survived the war, and they had not a penny to their names and no relatives left alive. They did what anyone back then would do - they went to America.

"Wir haben das memo über Israel nicht erhalten," grandad said, with a smile that looked a lot like grandson's.

Once again they found themselves living with two families in the same neighborhood, this time in New York. They found jobs, saved up their money, and when the time was right, he proposed.

She said yes, on one condition.

He said, "You name it" and she said, "We will never speak German in our home, only English, and our children and their children and all the children that ever come after will never speak German."

Grandson confirmed this, so I know it's true.

Grandad agreed, they got married, and grandson was the son of their first child. They had five children and twelve grandchildren, so far.

Not one of them speaks a lick of Deutsch.

We went on like that until they finally called me back.

There was something peaceful and sweet in his manner, and about our talk, that caused time to stop for a while. I think other people were listening. In fact, the receptionist sent somebody back before me that should have gone after me. I was fine with it.

In the short time we had together we conversed about shame, hatred, family, love, country, forgiveness, a few other things you wouldn't expect, and shoes. Sometimes indirectly, when to be direct wasn't possible.

From this conversation I learned an entire philosophy of shoes, which I believe to be solid to this day.

So, like I said, if I ask about your shoes, there's a reason.

Farewell, Hollywood

A body on the sidewalk was a common sight by the time I moved into the Roosevelt. Some weren't quite dead and would reach out at you, so it was best to walk in the street to keep your suit a little cleaner. The street was safe; the traffic had died with the people.

The dead littered the sidewalk like leaves in a New England fall, waiting to be collected. If nobody came, the thriving rat population got to work, a force multiplier for the plague.

The stench of excrement and pot smoke that hung over Hollywood Boulevard had been replaced by something far worse. I could always tell when it was time to replace my filters.

Before the plague, the Roosevelt Hotel had been converted into luxury flats. They were nice, but the Roosevelt had become inexpensive, in line with demand.

The glory of her restoration faded, along with the tenants and the rents. The papered walls and polished brass once again tattered and dull, dirty carpets removed. There was no one left to clean them and scant few left to care.

The Roosevelt had a decon chamber where its grand entrance once stood. You didn't take your suit off, just stepped in, got hosed, and you were all set. It was the last new thing in the building, notable for its regular maintenance.

I spent a lot of nights on the roof watching ships launch from Vandenberg. Once the rockets got going you could watch them burn their way to space, bound for Mars.

The colony went silent a year into the plague. People, myself included, thought for sure they'd abandon the place and bring everyone back home. Then one day Mars sent a message. Something like "Come to Mars, everything's hunky-dory."

The wealthy went first, pretty much emptied out L.A., then the price dropped. By the fifth year people were lining up to buy tickets.

When Davy got his chance, he bought a ticket of his own and left me the house, the furniture, the near-empty bank accounts, the cars, all of it. Signed it all over, said he didn't give a damn.

"If you change your mind, sell everything and come find me. The colony's not so big, you'll be able to track me down."

"I'll keep that in mind," was all I said. He walked through the airlock, climbed aboard the shuttle, and that was it. I tried to cry, but couldn't manage it.

That night I drove up the coast and into the mountains to watch. Four hundred feet of spacecraft, accelerating into the heavens, it blasted away with so much force it shook the earth beneath me and warmed the vibrating air around me.

Hadn't heard a peep out of Davy since.

A few months later they stopped flying out of Vandenberg altogether and only launched out of Florida. There was a time they talked about launching from Texas, but that never happened. Even in a dying world, not too many people wanted to drive to Boca Chica, and everybody knows location is everything.

Davy always had a nose for trouble. He sold his

investments early on, hoarded cash, then bought gold. Not paper gold. He went for coins, ingots, and bars. He kept everything in a safe he installed in the basement.

I used to say you never lost money on an investment until you sold it. I guess I learned my lesson. By the time I realized the whole damn game was over, well, it was over.

I was broke long before Davy left. We fought about it all the time. "I told you to unload that shit," Davy would scream at me.

"I didn't have a fucking crystal ball," I'd scream back.

"But I told you," is where he usually left it. He was right, but that didn't make it easier. He left me a stack of his coins to "tide me over," but I figured gold would be worthless like everything else before long. Wrong again.

When I did sell everything, it didn't fetch much. But when I moved into the Roosevelt, I felt a degree of security for the first time in years. That's when I decided to buy more gold.

I bought jewelry mostly, and I got pretty good at it. I didn't so much buy it as take it off dead bodies and leave a few greenbacks stuffed in a pocket. Nobody gave a damn anymore, so why not? It was easy enough to clean.

Then the price of gold went through the stratosphere and like that, I was flush again.

It helped I didn't have to buy food. The military would drop crates of MREs from a helicopter every so often. It had to be a mistake. What didn't go to the rats came mostly to me. I thought I'd won the lottery when one of those crates contained a case of filters for my breather. I could go out in comfort again.

Things were looking up for me at that point.

I stayed at the Roosevelt even after they shut down Vandy. I was one of the few paying tenants left, which made it easy to knock the price down when the time came.

For the next year I crawled the streets in my hazmat,

haunted the gold exchange, ate freeze-dried food, and spent nights on the roof drinking gin and staring at the stars.

Then my time was up. I dropped a few coins on a dying man for an electric truck with bulletproof glass, armor plating, high-density solar panels on the roof, and the best air scrubbers money could buy.

When I was loading up for my cross-country drive to Florida, piling cases of MREs into the truck bed, I wondered what they were eating up on Mars.

All those new arrivals, they must have figured something out.

Jacob's Well

The boy who died was not my friend. I knew him, but not well. The boy who lived was my friend, but after that night at Jacob's Well he was never the same. The joyful, good natured college student was replaced by a person sullen and withdrawn, one who lived in a perpetual state of darkness.

The girl wasn't physically harmed, but the deepest wounds are often hardest to see, and can take longer to heal. The totality of her role remains obscured. I know only what she told me, and that wasn't everything, I'm certain.

You might not think of Texas when you think of scuba diving. But if you spend enough time there, you'll hear stories about places like Canyon Lake, the San Marcos River, Spring Lake, and eventually Jacob's Well.

The Texas Hill Country is as named, rolling hills, tall grass, broad-branched oaks. Subterranean city-sized aquifers provide water to most of the region. Pressure from below sends water surging up through springs large and small, forming crystal clear streams and rivers that weave their way to the Gulf of Mexico, growing brown and murky along the way.

Jacob's Well was such a place. A fissure in the earth, a vertical opening a dozen feet in diameter at the surface. Water pushed up from a cavern system 150 feet below, gaining velocity along the way. It flows up through the widening well until it reaches the surface, then follows the path of least resistance at a languid pace, becoming Cypress Creek.

Persons lost to time built a concrete structure around two-thirds of the upper rim of the opening, an excellent place for swimmers to sit and stare into the depths, legs dangling in the water. To dive the well was to descend into utter darkness, traverse the connecting tube, and emerge into world few had ever seen, and fewer still lived to describe.

After the two divers perished in the aquifer, an iron grate was placed across the opening of the tube in an unsuccessful attempt to prevent further tragedy. The barrier was once again breeched, and more deaths soon followed. Not everyone knows their own limits, and those who do often seek to test them.

I'm not certain why the trio snuck across private land, gear in tow, late one Friday night with only the owls and coyotes to bear witness. At least Jan accepted her limits. She chose to remain on the surface rather than join Jason and Keith in the water.

Keith and Jason, like Jan, were juniors at State College. All of them had learned to dive at a local dive shop, the only one between San Antonio and Austin. That's where I met the three of them, and that's how Jason and I became friends.

Jason had his Divemaster certification, on the cusp of becoming an Instructor, along with a raft of specialty certifications, Search and Recovery, Night Diving, you name it, he went for it. But he never trained for cave diving. He had enough experience to know the dangers of it, but failed to factor in the exponential risk presented by the depth of an aquifer, when he set out for Jacob's Well.

The owner of the dive shop, Max, was a kind and generous man, but he was quiet, rarely making time for small talk. His combat experience as a Navy demolition diver, BUDS they called it, made him the first person called when a lake needed searching, a body needed recovering.

I was drawn to Jason and his mentorship. I could ask him anything and he would answer with his usual patience and good cheer. He was the reason I continued training, becoming a working Divemaster myself, with a list of certifications to my name, like him.

We had grown close by the time Jason took Keith and Jan to Jacob's Well. He told me later the whole thing had been his idea. In my mind, the genesis of the thing didn't matter once it was done.

The three of them lived together in a grand, decaying old house miles from campus. I assumed Jan and Keith were just roommates and friends. In retrospect, I wonder if there was more to it. Strange how time can both confuse and clarify such things. I had my secrets and they had theirs. Whatever the case, they didn't ask me to join them and I'm grateful they left me out of their plans.

There were no cell phones then, no internet, no email, no text messaging. When you wanted to talk to someone you either called them on a landline or you went to see them, if a letter was too slow.

When Jan showed up pounding on my door at 3:00 AM, I found myself opening it before I was fully awake. She rushed in, threw her arms around me, and buried her face in my chest. I couldn't make sense of what she was saying. I'd never seen her unhappy before, much less frantic and in tears. I led her to the kitchen and one of my roommates, Tim, came to see what was happening. She and I sat at the kitchen table and Tim poured glasses of water for each of us. This simple act allowed her a few moments to collect herself.

I asked her the expected questions, what was wrong, what was happening, was she all right. She took one long deep breath then exhaled, "I think Keith is dead."

My mind could not fully wrap itself around what she was telling me.

"Where's Jason?" I asked.

"Did you hear me? Keith is dead!"

"You said you think he's dead. Is Jason with him?"

She slammed her glass onto the table and glared at me. I looked her in the eyes, saw the anguish and the terror, her state of mind encapsulated in those bloodshot eyes, dark circles curving below, glistening with her tears. Her stare stopped me cold.

Tim took a seat between us and placed a hand on her arm. "Tell us what happened."

He was a lesson in kindness, empathy, and maturity I will never forget.

Jan looked at Tim as though she was seeing him for the first time. She wiped at her face and said, "I could use a tissue."

I retrieved a roll of paper towels and placed it on the table in front of her.

"Boys, you're all the same," she said. Something like a laugh escaped her before she began crying again.

She composed herself, then started to tell the story.

"We went to Jacob's Well," she began.

"Oh god, Jan, no…"

"I didn't go in, I was going to but…"

"But what?"

"Such a dumb idea, I don't know why I went with them, I told them it was stupid but they had to do it, with or without me, they just had to do it."

She took a long drink of water and continued, "We snuck in from the backside of the park. I looked down into that hole and I knew I couldn't do it. I stayed on the ledge, I watched their lights go down until I couldn't see them anymore. I thought it would be an hour, maybe less. I kept expecting to see their bubbles coming back up. But they never did."

"Are they still down there? We have to call Max," I felt a chill creep over my body. I knew we had to act, but couldn't pull myself from the table until I heard more. Whatever had happened, I was witnessing the aftermath, not the event.

Her voice dropped to a whisper, "I never saw the bubbles, then all of a sudden Jason is there, gasping for air. I had to pull him out of the water, he was a wreck. He kept saying, over and over, 'Get to a phone, call Max, go to his house if you have to, hurry, hurry.'

Max was accustomed to off-hours calls for help, usually from law enforcement. The phone at the shop automatically forwarded to his home when the business was closed.

"Have you talked to Max yet? Is Jason still there?"

"I left him at the well. He wouldn't leave. I went to a gas station on Route 4. It had a phone booth. I... I knew Keith was dead. I know it. There's no way... but I called the shop, Jason said to call Max, so I did."

She took a drink of water, her hand shaking enough to spill it down her chin. "He was so calm," she said, "he didn't get angry, didn't ask me a lot of questions. I must have been screaming into the phone and all he said was to go back to the well and wait. I don't know why I came here, I...I couldn't go back there..."

"You need to do as he said, you need to get back there," I said.

"What good would it do?" she asked, "I can't help them."

Tim sat back in his chair and looked at me. "You should drive her."

"Yes," she said, emphatically, "Please, I can't, I barely got here."

Dawn was creeping up along the horizon by the time we pulled through the open gate into a kaleidoscope of flashing lights from the police cars and emergency vehicles. We were stopped by a Texas Ranger. "What the hell are you two doin' here? Go on now, nothin' to see here."

When I explained our purpose, he told us where to wait. I parked and we exited the car. I saw Jason, wrapped in a blanket, seated on the tailgate of a pickup. I'd never seen him so forlorn. I wanted desperately to go to him. He was broken, his eyes down, his normally dark skin ashen, the whites of his eyes lost in an ocean of red and black. He didn't move, didn't look up, didn't speak. I was staring at him, lost in my own thoughts, when Max approached us, wetsuit peeled away from his upper body, long hair stuck in dark streaks to his shoulders and chest, pale skin stretched over lean muscle and thick bone.

"Charlie what the hell… what's your business in all this?"

"Nothing," I said, "I didn't think she should drive herself back out here alone, that's all."

"You can leave, I'll make sure she gets home, there's some folks here want to talk to her. You keep quiet 'bout this 'til I say otherwise, you hear me?"

"Sure, yes sir, anything I can do to help?"

"What's done is done. You wanna help out, you get on the phone and tell everybody you can get a hold of to be at the shop, noon today. Can you do that?"

"Yes sir, I can do that."

"Awright then, get a move on. Janice, come on with me."

He delivered Jan to group of Rangers waiting by the truck where Jason sat. Jason looked up and saw her, then me, his eyes lingering for a moment, a pleading look, then cast down again. I got in the car, Keith's car, and drove home. I spent the early hours after dawn calling every diver affiliated with the shop I could reach, delivering Max's message, and instructing them to pass it on.

I arrived at the dive shop 30 minutes early. Max's wife came to the locked door and spoke to me through the glass.

"You come about last night?" she asked.

"Yes m'am."

"What's your name?"

"Charlie. Max asked me to call everybody…"

"He told me 'bout you," she said. She unlocked the door and let me in, "go on back to the classroom. There's coffee an' biscuits, best git yourself some."

"Yes m'am, thank you."

The back half of the dive shop held a classroom and small indoor pool. I entered the classroom and saw Max sitting in a chair facing Jason. I couldn't hear what he was saying. Jason looked up from their conversation and Max turned around to see who it was. "You're early," he said, then left the room.

Jason stood up and hugged me. He didn't say a word, didn't cry, just wrapped his arms around me and held me. I returned the embrace, and did not want to let him go. But he eventually stepped back and looked at me. He was about to speak, changed his mind, and left the room.

Word of the meeting had spread farther than I expected. People began to arrive, each of them filled with questions. The message had been simple, Max wanted everyone at the shop, and it was important enough to forego other obligations.

The room grew noisy, until Max entered, bringing Jason, and silence, with him. He stood at a chalk board and surveyed the room. He turned to the blackboard, lifted a piece of chalk, and started to draw.

He traced two converging vertical lines, a large 'V,' the main body of Jacob's Well, then a pair of short horizontal lines, a narrow tube, moving at a downward angle away from the base of the wide vertical shaft. He then attached a large elliptical shape to the narrow tube but didn't close the far end. Someone said, "Oh shit."

We all knew what we were looking at, he'd

drawn it for every class, each time commanding us not to dive there. He wrote numbers on the diagram. A '0' at the top of the shaft, a '100' at the bottom, then, bearing down hard enough to splinter the chalk, a large '140' in the heart of the elliptical shape. He dropped what was left of the chalk and turned back to the room.

"Jason has something to say to y'all. Keep quiet and listen. Jason, you're up, talk loud so everybody can hear."

My face flushed red with anger at Max's cruelty, putting Jason on display, forcing him to explain what happened.

Jason stood at the board staring at the drawing. He turned to face the room, his eyes landing on me. Then he began to tell his story.

"Keith Wilson died last night," he said, "and it was my fault."

A few people started asking questions, some whispered to each other, the noise grew quickly.

"Ya'll be quiet, let the man speak," Max said. He didn't have to raise his voice, it cut naturally through the room like a river through a canyon. The room fell quiet. Jason cleared his throat and began to speak again.

"We heard Jacob's Well was open again, somebody pulled up the grate, we wanted to go see it. We went in before midnight. We got all the way in, all the way to the cavern. Somebody put a guide rope down there so we just followed it through. We saw something shiny in the silt. We dug it out, it was somebody's gear, an empty tank with a respirator, we got pretty excited about it. Then my light went out, it was damn dark in there. We tried to get out but the water… the silt we kicked up, you couldn't see anything with one light, so dark down there. The part where you have to take your tank off…"

"Jason, back up. Show 'em what happened," Max said, pointing at the blackboard.

Jason looked at Max, an unanswered cry for mercy. He

turned to the board and pointed at the most narrow section of the horizontal tube and continued, "Right about here, you have take off your tank and push it through in front of you, otherwise it's too narrow to get through. We stirred up a cloud of silt on the way in. On the way out I went through first. A little ways along it opens up enough to put your tank back on, right about here. I was doin' that, tryin' to put my gear back on, when Keith came through. I couldn't see a damn thing, Keith started pushin' on me, grabbin' me. I was tryin' to get my vest back on. I pushed against him, I could feel his wetsuit. He'd come through without his gear. Didn't have his vest so I knew he lost his tank. I tried to buddy breathe with him but he kept grabbin' at my mask. I couldn't see shit. I got his hand on my respirator, I know he got one good breath, maybe two, then I had to pull it back from him, but he wasn't havin' it. He wouldn't let go and kept shovin' me down into the bottom, into the silt. I dropped my light. It took both hands... I got the respirator back from him but hardly got a breath before he pulled it away from me again."

Jason paused, still facing away from us. He took a few deep breaths, then turned around to face us.

"I lost it. I knew my tank was close to empty. Y'all know how depth steals your air, crushes it down to nothin' and we were deep, hundred, hundred-twenty feet. I guess it came down to him or me or both of us. I turned my back to him and he kept clawin' at me. He got my mask off, I couldn't see, I was just scrapin' in the silt tryin' to get away from him. Next thing I know I got that rope in my hand and I'm pullin' for dear life as hard as I could and all of a sudden he wasn't pullin' on me anymore 'cuz he pulled my tank right off my back, took my breather along with it and I didn't stop pullin' on that rope, kickin' my feet for all I was worth, just pullin' for dear life."

He looked at the floor and paused, then looked up at us. "I

just wanted to get outta there, I didn't think of nothin' else, just get outta that goddamn hole and never look back."

When he stopped talking, the room remained quiet, but I knew I wasn't the only one trying not to cry.

"Grace," Max said, "how 'bout you take Jason to my office for a bit."

Grace had been standing in the door, watching and listening. She placed an arm around Jason and said, "Come on hun, you don't need to hear this part."

Jason looked up at Max, then at me. I could see the tears in his eyes, could feel my own forming. They left the room and Max returned to the blackboard. He lifted another piece of chalk and amended his diagram with a single narrow inverted cone rising up from the horizontal tube, terminating below the surface. He drew a circle around the closed top of the cone and a '30' beside it, then tossed the chalk away and turned back to the room.

"That right there, that spot," he said, "that's where I found him. For those that don't know it, that's called a false chimney. These aquifers are full of 'em and Jacob's Well ain't no different. You heard the story, I don't need to tell you he panicked." Max's voice began to rise, his anger boiling to the surface. "You are your own worst enemy when you are under water. If you don't know what the hell you're doin' then by God you shouldn't be doin' it."

Max let his words sink in and his anger cool by a few degrees.

"Keith's ain't the first body I've pulled from that place, but it's damn sure the last. Any of you get the bright idea to go down in that hole, you're as likely as Keith to die there. When that happens and your parents come to me, beggin' me to get you outta there, I'm gonna say no, and I'm not gonna bother explainin' myself. Hell, I damn near died down there pullin' another fool outta that place, some a y'all know that story, I got the scars to prove it. That boy should be at home havin' lunch right now, or out playin' ball, or doin' whatever the hell any of you probably wish you were doin' instead of sittin' in here. But he's not, and never will again. Y'all think about that and you think about this." Max swiveled his head back toward the blackboard and stabbed his finger at the circle he'd just drawn, then jerked his head back to us. He punctuated his words with stabs at the board, shaking it against the paneled wall, his anger regaining its force as he spoke.

"When he got to the end of that chimney, when that hole kept gettin' smaller and he hit solid rock, he didn't turn and go back down, he couldn't 'cuz he was too damn scared to think. No, he kept pushin' and clawin' and diggin' like he was gonna bust through the Earth and find himself some air, like he was sure if he just jammed himself up there some more he'd break through. Tore his fingernails off, smashed his face, wedged himself in so tight we had to put a rope on his legs and pull him down. Y'all think about that next time you wanna do somethin' damn foolish. I didn't start this business so I could pull the dead bodies of any a y'all outta the water. This shit didn't have to happen, y'all know that's the truth."

When he stopped shouting the room remained quiet and still.

Until I raised my hand.

"What is it Charlie?"

I could tell by the way he spat out the words he didn't want any questions, but I had one I needed to ask.

I looked around the room, the blank expressions of people, most I'd never met, staring back at me. I turned back to Max. "Maybe it can wait."

"I bet it can," Max replied, his voice rising at first, then falling back to a more indoor volume, "Y'all go on home. Charlie, you wanna be useful, stick around and help me with my gear."

"Yes sir."

Max watched the assemblage of students and former students file out. Exhaustion and sadness overcame me and I lowered my face into my hands. I sat like that until I felt a hand on my shoulder. I looked up to see Max standing over me. I felt my lips quiver and the tears begin to fall.

"It's gonna be alright," he said. "Come on, we got some work to do."

"I gotta ask, something ain't right…"

"There ain't nothin' right…"

I took a deep breath, composed myself, "The light," I said, not certain I wanted to know the truth, but certain I was going to ask for it, "if his light went out, how did he go through the squeeze first? He's my friend, my best friend, but that…."

Max shook his head, cutting me off, "Charlie, if that's the truth, if he's your best friend, then the best you can do for him is let this go."

"But…"

"No buts, you let it go. One boy is dead, another might as well be. He's gonna need us, all of us, to help him get some kinda life back. You aren't the only smart kid in the room, somebody else is probably thinkin' the same thing you are. And I'd tell 'em the same thing I'm gonna tell you. It doesn't matter how it went down, it went down. Casting blame, right or wrong, won't bring Keith home. The best we can do is salvage whats left of the mess they made."

"Okay,…okay," I said. I was stunned by the realization the story we'd heard was a lie.

Max moved his hand to my knee and leaned in, forcing me to look into his bloodshot eyes, filled with tears, "Listen Charlie," he began, his voice choked with pain, "I am sick and tired of talking about Jacob's Well to a bunch of kids who don't fuckin' listen. This time, I have a survivor, not a dead body no one's ever gonna see. I made a lesson of him, and he's gonna own that lesson the rest of his life. That's the deal, that's what we came up with. Maybe it's right, maybe not, but sometimes you gotta take what you can get. Sometimes the truth can do more harm than it's worth. You understand what I'm tellin' you?"

I sensed someone else in the room and looked over my shoulder to see Jason standing inside the doorway, a mirror image of my early arrival for the meeting. Exhaustion, fear, cold, maybe all of those things combined, he was shaking, wringing his hands, looking at me like a drowning man waiting for a life rope.

"I understand."

"All right then, come on out here and help me unload the truck."

Jason backed out of the room and stood aside as we walked out. He reached out and put a hand on my arm. I looked at him and realized I would never see him the same way again. I also knew it wasn't my place to judge him. I could not know if I would have behaved any different, had I been in his place. Then again, I'd never wanted to dive Jacob's Well.

I waited for him to speak. He seemed he was about to when Max called back, "Come on Charlie, truck won't unload itself."

I took a step and felt Jason's hand move, "Thank you," he said, a notch above a whisper.

I reached back, touched his shoulder, and kept on walking.

I realized Max was right, Keith was not the only one who died that night.

We unloaded the truck; while Jason took the wet gear to the drying racks near the pool, Max and I stowed the tanks and ropes and other equipment in their proper places. We didn't speak another word, but that work was some kind of occupational therapy for all of us. When we finished, I drove Jason to my place in Keith's car. I expected him to drive himself home from there.

We pulled into the drive and before I got out he asked, "Can I stay for a little while?"

"Jan's alone in that big-ass house of yours…"

"I know. She and Keith, they…" his voice trailed off.

"You don't want to see her, or she don't want to see you?"

Jason stared down at the floorboard. "Both," he said, still speaking in a half whisper.

"Of course you can stay. You want a hot shower, something to eat?"

"Shower, that'd be nice."

I got out of the car and he didn't move. I leaned back in, "You comin'?"

He hesitate, then got out of the car and followed me inside. I pulled a towel from the hall closet. "You know where it is, take your time," I said and handed him the towel.

I tossed a pillow and a blanket on the sofa, along with a pair of sweatpants and a t-shirt. I assumed Jason was as ready as I was for some sleep. If he was hungry, he could help himself. I went into my bedroom and fell onto the bed, staring up at the popcorn ceiling. The house was silent other than the sound of the running water. I dozed off before the water stopped, then woke up when I heard Jason in the living room, then walking down the hall.

He stood in the hall, looking in at me. I didn't know what to say to him. I wanted to sleep and talk some other time. He came into the room and crawled into bed with me. He put his head on my chest, his arms around my shoulders. I put my arms around him. He turned away from me and began to sob. I pulled him close to me, his back pressed against me, my forehead against the nape of his neck. His body shook, chest heaved and fell, he cried as if his soul was dying. He wrapped his arms over mine and squeezed. He became lost in his sorrow, as deep as the well that had nearly claimed him, until the day's toll caught up with him and he fell asleep in my arms. It wasn't long before I was asleep as well.

Around sunset I heard the front door open and close, Tim arriving home from work. I heard his keys land on the kitchen table, then his footsteps down the hall. My back was to the door, I didn't turn around or move. He stopped at the open door for a moment, then continued down the hall.

I untangled my arms from Jason, careful not to wake him. I went to the living room, rolled a joint, grabbed a beer from the fridge, and went to the patio to watch the sunset. Tim came out and sat next to me. I handed him the joint, he took a good long pull and held it in, handing the joint back to me.

"You hot-boxed it again Timmy, told you not to do that."

He let the smoke out slow and steady, speaking as he exhaled, "Sorry bud, long day, ready to get a buzz on."

"You're telling me."

He leaned back in his chair, threatening to topple it over backwards, then let himself rock forward. "You and him, you guys…"

"It's not like that."

"But you're like that."

"Like what?"

"Queer."

"I think the word you're looking for is gay. I'm gay. Is it that obvious?"

"Not from a distance. But you don't date, people notice. This the first time you said it out loud?"

"I suppose it is."

"I'm honored. Why now?"

I handed him the joint again. "Because life is too short to keep living in a closet."

"You're in small town Texas, bud, I suggest you keep livin' that way. But don't worry, you're in good company." He grinned, and took another long drag.

"What are you saying?"

He cocked his head to one side, held the joint up to the air, exhaled and said, "Birds of a feather Charlie, birds of a feather."

He handed the joint back to me and rocked back in his chair again, still smiling at me.

"Well I'll be damned," I said, and despite the nature of the day, found myself smiling back. "Nothing like a little revelation to brighten a dark day. The other fellas know about…"

"Of course," he said, and reached his hand out for the stub of the joint, "why you think they let you move in with us?"

"All this time…you ain't never said a word…I will be damned. Why now? Today of all…"

"I saw you in there, with him, figured it was ad good a time as any to bring it up. Guess I was only half right." He inhaled as deep as he could, held the smoke in for a while, then slowly let it out, nostrils flaring, smoke pouring out each side, like a cartoon bull.

"Half right, all right, doesn't matter much at this point. I'll say this much, your timing sucks."

"Better late than never. Why don't you go wake your boy up, see if he wants to join us."

I gave it some thought, then said, "No, I don't think I will. He needs the sleep. Besides, I think me and him are gonna be walkin' different paths from here on out."

"Just like that, you cut him loose."

"Not cuttin' him loose. I've followed him around like a lost puppy for more than a year. Turns out, he's more lost than me, even more so now. After today, I'm thinkin' I can find better things to do with my time."

Tim laughed and rose from his chair, unsteady at first. He shook his head, let out a chuckle, and patted my shoulder, letting his hand linger there, looking down at me. "You hold that thought right there, I'm gonna roll us up another one, and we can talk some more about this path of yours."

He went inside and left me to stare out at the rolling hills beyond the wire fence across our back yard, the sunset burning golden in the distant trees. In the silence, I found myself wondering what else I didn't know about my world and the people in it, what other secrets and mysteries there were for me to uncover. It occurred to me, I might now be the one heading down a dark tunnel, into the unknown. And if that were the case, I could only hope I was prepared for whatever lay ahead.

The Road West

Sometimes we learn things which seem useless when we learn them, like algebra or French, only to discover at some later point those things can be decidedly useful. When I was a kid I learned the hard way it only takes a few pounds of pressure to dislocate your elbow. I was eleven and a bicycle accident landed me in the hospital with a concussion and, you guessed it, a dislocated elbow. The doctor felt it was important I know how easy it is for an elbow to get damaged, a few pounds of pressure, ten to be precise, and the elbow gave way. I couldn't see the point at the time. Little did I know how important his tidbit would be a decade later, during a strange time in my life in Texas.

Interstate I-10, between San Antonio and El Paso is long, flat, and generally straight. Variations are rare enough to cause accidents as drivers, lulled into complacency by the endless sameness of the desert of Southwest Texas, suddenly find themselves navigating a curve or an unexpected off-ramp.

It was no place to stop at night. If you did, to fix a flat for instance, you were running the risk of someone rolling up on you in the dark. One might mistake the open space for an unpopulated place. That would be a deadly mistake. There were people out there all right, and they were not often the friendly "let me help you change your tire" type.

If you had to make the run west from Austin, via San Antonio, as I did from time to time, you damn sure better travel in daylight and plan ahead. Unless of course you had a reason to travel in the dark. Four bricks of the purest cocaine I'd ever laid eyes on gave me plenty of reason to break my own travel rules, so a night drive it was. Besides, I'd grown up on a steady diet of Mad Max re-runs at the dollar theater, I knew how to prepare.

I can't say it was something I'd never done before, the drug trade, but this particular run to El Paso was a big step up for me. Or down, depending on your perspective. I'd been small time for a long time, by design. Mostly pot, the occasional eight ball or two. You might say the latter set me on my current path.

Previous trips usually involved bags of pot, sometimes cash, not bricks of coke. But I have always been the pragmatic sort. The "you do this for us, we won't do this to you" kind of pragmatism that kept one both alive and out of jail, a win-win logic. Trade one evil for another, one terrible decision for a less terrible one. I suppose my arrangement wouldn't matter to a judge if I happened to get caught, at least not in the short term. I wasn't worried about getting caught, I'd been down that road before. I was worried about missing my offramp and having to make a u-turn through the median. The '82 Impala sedan I was driving wasn't built for off-roading and the likely outcome would be to get stuck between the east- and west-bound lanes. Vigilance was my word of the day.

To the uninitiated, it might seem I was going the wrong direction, from Texas toward a rendezvous in Mexico. That would be correct most of the time, but drug lords work in mysterious ways, and the shortest path is not always the most direct, especially for high-risk product.

My goods came in through the Port of Houston, part of a much larger load slipped into the country inside a container of coconuts or ceramics or some other such items hollowed out and sealed up again. My little bundle was a drop in the bucket.

I'd drop my package, pick up a bag of cash, then drop the cash in Juarez. The border guards were less vigilant on the way into Mexico and they usually knew which cars to ignore. My ride stood out for the horns strapped across the bashed in grill.

I'd have another two stops after Juarez before I could turn toward home. Meanwhile, the package would make its way to the next leg of its journey via some ambitious young soldiers stationed at Fort Bliss, with easy access to well-protected air transportation. I wasn't supposed to know all the details, but I did, so there it is.

I got the higher paying job because of previous experience, lucky me. I didn't mind the ten hours of solitude, but the shitty music tested my mettle. The car's audio system consisted of an AM radio blasting through a dried out speaker in the dashboard, old-school country until one station after another fell out of range and some godawful preacher took the place of the music, screaming about hellfire and brimstone and the end of days, which, to my mind, couldn't come fast enough once the screaming started.

Off-ramps are a tricky thing. There aren't many and most of the traffic signs get stolen or hit with so many shotgun blasts they deteriorate to not much more than crumbling rust, illegible to the point of pointlessness. It was hard enough to spot them in the daylight, those places where a nearly invisible road, often times gravel, intersected the interstate and the highway rose up enough to let the locals pass beneath it.

My interim destination, the rendezvous point, was a

smudge of a road called "The Boulevard" smack dab in the middle of nowhere, the byproduct of a failed land development scam. I suppose for the developers it was some form of success. Again, it's all about perspective.

A quick stop, swap packages, and I'd be done with the more dangerous part of my trip. Getting off the highway, and parking under it at night, swapping drugs for cash, added up to a sketchy maneuver, even for me. I convinced myself everything would be fine, but out of an abundance of caution I aimed to be a bit late. I'd rather piss off the other guy, assuming it was a guy, than sit there like a turd in pool waiting to get spotted.

The plan was simple. Hit the off-ramp, bang a left, flash my lights three times, then money would fall from the sky. I'd make the exchange and be on my merry way to Juarez to meet my south-of-the-boarder associates. Scoot back north across the bridge for a check-in with the real boss, the one pulling all the strings. The one who scared me the most, and therefore was kept as happy as possible. It seemed like a good plan to me.

Unfortunately, the other side of the equation decided on a different set of steps.

I fueled up in Fort Stockton, a 'last chance for gas' kind of place and grabbed myself the largest cup of coffee they sold. About forty miles further, I-10 met up with its northern cousin, I-20, and from there it wasn't much more than an hour to my appointed stop. I assumed there'd be guns involved in the transaction. I hated guns, but I knew my way around them better than most. I wasn't carrying anything more dangerous than a lock blade knife, which I kept it in the trunk with the junk. Still, I'd learned from ol' Max and his trusty dog how to be ready for anything. I had a surprise of my own up my sleeve if I needed one.

I was right on time, my time anyway. A pair of rusty poles

stood in for a road sign. One of the poles sported a series of flashy reflective stripes, two yellow and one white. My sign to exit. So far, so good.

I flipped off the headlights and was damn thankful for the light of the crescent moon and the clear night sky. I tapped the brakes and dropped down the ramp at a leisurely pace. I blew the stop sign, swung into the intersection, and aimed toward the overpass. I spotted a car on the left, facing me, resting beyond the shadows. Guess they didn't realize the moon moved with the clock. Criminals, bunch of morons when you get down to it.

I flashed my lights as instructed, revealing a man, pale as a ghost, sitting in the driver's seat. He hit me back with a single flash. I eased up next to him and rolled down my window.

He flicked his cigarette butt out his window, bouncing it off my car door. Great, seven hours on the road and they send an asshole to meet me.

"You Charlie?" he asked.

"Yup, you Bert?"

"You don't need ta know my name, turn ya car 'round 'n pull on up behind me."

I rolled forward, then performed the worst multi-point turn of my life. By the time I got sorted out, my counterpart was standing in the road next to his open door.

That's when I figured out he was a lefty - the pistol in his hand was a dead giveaway.

Not good. If he's already drawn the damn thing, he's either dumb as a brick, scared as hell, about to rip me off, or some combination of the three. My money was firmly on the last bet. I put the car in park and rested my hands on the steering wheel.

"Keep ya hands where I can see 'em," he shouted, apparently unable to see my hands where he could see them. I flipped on the interior light, then wiggled my hands in the air to make extra sure he saw them. I should have been scared, but I wasn't. It happened to me sometimes, the emotions shut down, things move in slow motion. It came naturally to me, which probably meant it was a bad thing. In this case, I knew staying calm would at least preserve my dignity, if not my life.

He raised his weapon and walked toward me shouting, "Open the trunk," as if I were a mile away. Dumb, unscrupulous, and scared - the trifecta. I wasn't expecting a mastermind in the desert, but this guy was a mess.

"I can't open it from here, switch is broken, gotta get out," I replied, hoping my backup plan hadn't fallen off somewhere along the road.

"Show me," he shouted. He aimed his gun at my head and stepped closer. "Nothin' funny, ya hear me, I'll blow your fuckin' head clean off, you got it?"

I decided it was a good time to bring out the Texas drawl I'd picked up since moving to Austin. It couldn't hurt. "You ain't gotta scream, I'm sittin' right here," I said.

"I'll scream if I wanna," he said, his voice rising a full octave, "now open the goddam truck."

"It don't work, watch." I reached down to pull the latch and he jerked his pistol closer to my head. I put my hands back up and gave him a second to catch his breath, then slowly moved my left hand down. I kept my eyes on him so I had to feel around to find the t-shaped handle. I made a show of pulling on it a few times so he'd get the message.

"Fine," he said, this time using his indoor voice, "git out," and waved his weapon toward the back of the car.

"You know this is a bad idea," I said as I shut off the car and got out, "people are waiting for me in Juarez, they won't take kindly to me being late, 'specially since I ain't never late."

"Shut the fuck up and open the trunk."

"You're a poet and didn't know it," I quipped. Sometimes I couldn't help myself.

He annunciating every word, "I said shut up and open the fuckin' trunk," which made me wonder if I'd laid on the redneck twang a little too thick. He might think I'm an idiot, which, under the circumstance, would be hard to refute.

But momma didn't raise no fool.

He stepped further away and walked in a wide arc as I went to the back of the car and moved to slide the key into the lock. I fiddled with the keys and dropped them, then kicked them a little ways under the car. It was an award-winning performance, if I do say so myself.

"Shit, man, you got a flashlight by any chance? I can't see a damn thing under there."

"What the fuck is wrong with you? You some kinda shit-for-brains for damn sure." He reached into his pocket, retrieving a lighter and tossing it at me.

"The gas tank is right there and you want me to light a fire under it? And you think I'm shit for brains?"

"Stop fuckin' around and get the goddam trunk open!"

"Okay, okay, don't get your panties in a wad," I said. I knelt down and started flicking the lighter. I thought I heard something, a soft kind of swooshing sound, from somewhere behind me, a car passing overhead maybe. I dismissed it and focused on the search for the errant keys.

"There they are, I see 'em, gotta reach a little.. shit, damn, fire!" I dropped the lighter, pretending it burned my thumb, then reached above the keys and grabbed my can of bear spray. I'd learned all about bear spray in the Boy Scouts. I kept a can stashed next to the gas tank for occasions such as the one I was facing. Never had to use it before, guess there really is a first time for everything.

A quick tug on the canister and a flash of inspiration strikes. In an instant I realized how useful it was to know it only takes ten pounds of force to snap a man's elbow backwards. Apply the right amount of pressure at the right spot and you'd render an arm useless. Ten pounds, if you could get close enough.

Bear spray to the rescue. I started to rise but instead of standing up I swung my left hand out and unleashed a heavy stream of noxious liquid. It didn't have to be perfect, anywhere near the eyes would do, but I guess I was lucky. The stream hit him right in the mouth. And his mouth was open, so yeah, bullseye.

He fell back and gagged and again I got lucky, he didn't pull the trigger right away. I drop the can, grabbed his left hand with mine, and dropped my pinky finger in front of the revolver's hammer. He pulled the trigger and the hammer snapped down with an audible crunch. Losing a finger but not getting shot, a trade I'll make every day and twice on Sunday. I gripped with all my strength, the pistol and my hand became one and the same, white on rice.

He was gagging and puking, blowing snot everywhere, trying to stay on his feet and in the process jerking his hand away from me. But I wasn't trying to get the gun from him, not yet. I kept my bloody death grip on his weapon, pulled his arm toward me and gave it a twist to lock it up, then slammed my right hand right through his elbow with a hell of a lot more than ten pounds of force.

The sound of that joint snapping backwards was beautifully disgusting. He managed to scream between wretches, at which point I took his gun from him like, as they say, candy from a baby. He fell to the ground and screamed some more, trying to make sense of what had happened to his arm, snot pouring from both nostrils, his eyes beet red, his tongue and lips swelling to the point of forcing him, at long last, to shut up.

I took my time extracting my finger from the pistol, held it in my right hand, then pointed it at his pathetic face. I didn't see any reason to shoot him, he was beyond being a threat by then. I worried he might not survive the bear spray, given how much of a taste he got.

"You got my money in your car or you come out here with nothin' but your dick in your hand? Nod your head if it's yes, say your fuckin' prayers if it's a no."

He may have tried to nod his head, hard to say. He was running out of consciousness. I hated the thought of searching his car. I didn't have time for it.

Then, like the arrival of the Angel Gabriel himself, a roaring engine to my left, and the world filled with a blinding white light. I held my bloody hand in front of my eyes, trying to block out enough light to see what I was dealing with. From beyond the blazing glory of what appeared to be a series of spotlights attached to the roof of the world's biggest pickup truck came a man's voice, "You gonna shoot him or not?"

I looked down at the wrecked body of my adversary, then, placing my bloody hand back in front of my eyes replied, "I don't know yet. Truth be told, I'd rather not."

"I'd rather you not shoot him too," the voice said "Matter of fact, I'd rather not shoot you. Why don't you set the gun on the trunk of the car and we can talk about this like civilized folks. You seem like a smart fella, you know I got the drop on you, I ain't gotta be civilized if you don't want it to go that way."

"I reckon all we got to talk about is whether or not you're gonna shoot me when I put the gun down," I said. I knew it was pointless, of course the voice wasn't bluffing. Everybody in Texas, except me most of the time, was armed and more than ready to pull the trigger

"If your name is Charlie, and I'm thinking it is, then I got no cause to shoot you. Put down the gun and let's talk this through, maybe you can live to see another day."

I thought about it for a second, looked back down at Bert, who by then could barely manage to wheeze and gag, then into the light. "Okay, I'm puttin' down the gun."

I raised the weapon into the air, then laid it on the wide flat trunk of the car. I raised my hands up and asked, "Think you can dim the lights now?"

"Momma," the voice said, "kill the spots please."

All but one light shut off, then the cab lights switched on and I could see the man attached to the voice. He was standing a few feet from the passenger side of the truck. Smart cookie this one. If I'd fired off a round I wouldn't have come close. A woman occupied the driver's seat. They looked like grandparents. Grandpa was holding a shotgun, aimed at me, which he lowered, then walked towards me. The women got out and joined him.

"Howdy," the man said, "my name's Bert 'n this here's Ethel, my wife. Sorry we're late, we missed the dang ramp, had to bushwhack back. Looks like we come up on ya in the nick a time."

"If you're Bert, who the hell is this guy," I said, gesturing at the man on the ground.

"Don't know," the woman, Ethel, replied, "but we got a purty good idea who he works for, and it ain't us."

"Pardon my French m'am, but what the fuck is going on?"

"No offense hun, I heard plenty worse. Seems we got what you call a leak in our little operation. Sure do appreciate you helpin' us plug it," she said, a smile as big as Texas across her face.

"Listen now, I don't mean to be pushy or nothin'," Bert, the real Bert, said, "but it's gettin' late and we got a sitter with the grandkids tonight, so if you don't mind, I'd like to git down to business. You got a package for us?"

"I didn't come all this way for nothin', you got a package

for me?"

"Of course we do hun," Ethel said, still smiling, "this ain't our first rodeo. You fetch our package and I'll go fetch yours, sound good?"

"Yes m'am, it's right here in the trunk" I said, pointing at the trunk with my blood soaked hand.

"Momma, grab the first aid kit while you're back there, let's see if we can fix young Charlie's hand up, until he can get it looked at someplace."

"Okay," she called back over her shoulder.

"I'll need to move the pistol before I open the trunk," I said.

"Sure, you go right ahead," Bert said and shifted the barrel of his shotgun enough to aim it at my crotch. He cracked a smile and made a little motion with his head.

I picked up the pistol with two fingers, like I was picking up a dead mouse by the tail. "You want this or should I toss it into the bushes?"

"You can hand it to me if you like, no reason to throw out a perfectly fine piece."

He took the gun from me and shoved it inside his belt. I picked up the keys and opened the trunk. Ethel returned with a cloth bag and a metal box. I reached into the trunk with my good hand and lifted the four kilo bundle up by a strap made of duct tape, then held it out to Ethel.

She tossed the bag into the trunk and slammed the lid down, showing remarkable strength for a grandmother. "Set it on the ground hun, let me take a look at your hand, sit back on the trunk here." She placed the first aid kit on the trunk and with the skill of a battlefield medic, had my hand cleaned and bandaged in no time, complete with a tiny splint for my crushed pinky.

"You get yourself to a doctor, soon as you can," she said and patted me on my thigh when she finished her work, "you don't want no infection. The bone looks like it might need some refittin' too, help it knit proper."

"Yes m'am," I said, then pointed at the fake Bert. "What about him?"

"Don't you worry none about him, you jus' help me git him in the truck," Bert said, "we'll take it from here. You mosey on to Juarez, our friends down there get worried when folks run late, and you must be runnin' purty late by now."

"Yes sir, I guess I am. Thank you, ma'm, for this," I said, lifting my bandaged hand.

"No need to thank me hun, if we'd a been on time none of this woulda happened. But you did good tonight, real good," Ethel said, smiling sweetly. "You know," she continued, then looked at Bert, "next time we should have you up to the house for dinner, you could even stay the night, wouldn't that be nice Bert?"

"Yeah I reckon it would be nice," Bert said to her, then to me he said, "she makes the world's best chicken fried steak, you like chicken fried steak?"

I hated chicken fried steak. "Yes sir," I said, "love it, eat it every chance I get."

"It's settled, next time we'll skip all the skullduggery and have a nice dinner and some cold beer and git ta know each other a little better. I'm so happy how things is workin' out," Ethel said.

"Yes m'am," I said, "Me too."

"Awright now, before you go, gimme a hand with this one, Momma's strong but this ain't work for ladies."

"Yes sir," I replied.

"You are such a nice young man," Ethel said, "so polite, your momma raised you right, I'll say. You're a credit to her, ain't it so. Now you be careful with your hand, don't you go mess up all my good work."

"Grab him by the color, like this, next to me, we ain't gotta be gentle, let's get him in the bed of the truck and you can be on your way."

Together we managed to get fake Bert, the now unconscious, possibly near death, certainly soon to be dead, fake Bert, into the bed of Real Bert's truck while Ethel watched on, smiling her approval. When it was done she hugged me, a gentle grandmotherly but-not-my-grandmother hug, then we said our goodbyes, Ethel reminding me "Next time we'll meet up at the house, our boy in Austin can git you the directions. It'll be real nice to have you, I'll send word to our friends we'll be changin' up plans next time. Don't you worry 'bout nothin'." I said my last "yes m'am," got into the Impala and drove away as Real Bert got into Fake Bert's car.

An hour outside El Paso I pulled into an empty rest stop. It had an outhouse-style bathroom and these absurd 20 foot tall metal teepees over picnic tables, the ultimate in cultural appropriation. I nearly puked from the stench when I walked into the latrine. I gagged and retreated back into the night and made do in the shadows behind the cinderblock structure.

I bought two bottles of soda from an ancient vending machine, surprised and grateful they were cold.

Also to my surprise, the payphone worked. I stepped into the booth, closed the door and the light came on. I picked up the handset and breathed a sigh of relief when I heard the tone. I had no change, so I called collect, knowing Tim would accept the charges, but unsure he'd pick up the phone.

He answered on the first ring, and as expected accepted the call.

"Where are you?" he asked in a rush, "I've been worried..."

"I'm not there yet," I said, "little hiccup in the handoff."

"Hiccup? Charlie, you can't be late, you know..."

"It's fine, it's handled, I'm calling now because I won't get another chance for a while."

"Charlie, what the hell? What do you mean handled? What's going on?"

"Nothing's going on Timmy, a little confusion at the drop, nothing more, don't worry…"

"God, Charlie, I'm so sorry I got you into this, please…"

"You didn't get me into this, we got ourselves into this and we are getting ourselves out of it. Try to relax, you sound terrible."

"I am terrible. I sit by the phone and have these terrible thoughts."

"Then stop sitting by the phone. Go for a walk, make some dinner, go to a movie."

"No way, not until you're back here, safe and sound."

"It won't be long, a couple of days, you'll see. Then we'll go down to Padre and spend some of our ill-gotten gains. We can pop over to Matamoros, get us a nice steak dinner, soup to nuts, if you want."

"None of this feels right."

"You're telling me."

"I'm sorry…"

"Don't say sorry. There's no more sorry, there's you and me and a job we gotta do, that's it, you hear me? We'll get through this."

There was a long silence before he said, "You promise?"

"Yeah," I said, "yeah, I promise. Sooner or later, this will be over and we'll get on with our lives. Maybe we'll look back at this and laugh."

"It's gonna be a long time before I can laugh at anything."

"That's okay," I said, "I'm plannin' for us to have a long time to get there. You and me, together, all-in."

"You mean it?"

"Of course I do." I paused and I know he heard me take a deep breath and let it out. "I love you Timmy."

"You've never said that to me. Something's wrong."

"No Timmy, come on. Maybe I thought you sayin' it was enough for both of us. But…I don't know, I…I wanted you to hear it from me, for me to say it to you. We're gonna get through this, they can't hold this crap over our heads forever…"

"Yes, they can."

"I won't let them. Look, I gotta go, so I'll say it again, I love you. Now stop worrying and get some rest."

"Yeah, sure, I'll try. When will you call again?"

"Three days, maybe four."

"Okay, four days, I'll stop worrying in four days. I love you Charlie, but you knew that."

"Yeah, I did. I do. Four days, no more."

I hung up the phone before he could say any more. He could go on for hours, I didn't have the time.

I sat in the car with the engine off until the implications of what had happened at the overpass caught up to me. I started pounding the wheel, then the dash, the door, the seat, anything in range. Over and over again I beat the car with my good hand until it didn't feel like a good hand anymore. I couldn't stop. "Shit, goddammit, shit," I screamed into the emptiness of the night. When I'd spent my energy I opened one of my drinks, took a deep swig.

"Next time" I whispered, "what the hell, next time…"

I got out of the car and looked up at the blanket of stars above me, the moon hanging to the west, jagged outline of the mountains ahead of me. I thought about the decisions I'd made leading me to that moment, reminded myself there were more ahead. I considered running for it, take any road but the one I was on, but I knew West was my only way out.

I got back in the car, started the engine, and eased back onto the highway.

"Fuck it. In for a dime, in for a dollar." I jammed the

accelerator to the floor. Eight cylinders belched to life and I was flying. A ticket was the least of my worries. I had time to make up, and plenty of gas to burn.

Fitting In

As a boy, I longed to speak like the other boys I met when we moved to Georgia. My parents divorced when I was 4, and my earliest memories are blissful and dreamlike days and nights on my grandparent's farm in Iowa, early dawn hours of sweet air laced with dew, drifting in with the birdsong through the open window by the bed I shared with my uncle. He was eight, and my moon and stars. I was parked there for a year while my mother went out of state to work and figure out how to make a new life as a single mother. She married a man in Texas, and his job took us from Houston to New Orleans, then landed us in Georgia, just outside Atlanta.

We got to Georgia as I was starting third grade. A teacher decided there was something wrong with the way I talked, so they set me up with a speech therapist. I don't know what they set out to fix, but I could take a guess. All I know is I wanted to sound like all the other kids.

The boys in Georgia would say things like "ain't" or "dang-it" or "fixin-to" or "crik" and I soaked it up like the earth soaks up the sun. My mother had no intention of raising what she called "a redneck kid."

"You won't go anywhere in life if you don't speak proper English," she would say. I never dared ask her what that said about her new husband, the man I called "dad," and his

Texas drawl.

I secretly cataloged the Southern-isms I heard and by high-school I could pass as a native, at least among those who didn't know the truth. It felt good, those times I was anonymous, and could drop into the drawl and twang at will and be accepted like any other kid.

It had other uses too, like the time a cop pulled me over for speeding. "Awright young man, I'm gonna write you a warnin' this time, but I ketch you drivin' hell-bent for leather agin an' I'm writin' ya for real, ya unnerstan'?"

"Yes,sir, I do, you ain't never gonna see my face agin, off'sir, I swear."

I could start a new job and slip into a conversation with the other employees without anyone asking me "Where you from boy?"

Living this dual-dialect life also came in handy as training for how to deal with bigger problems. Like being gay at a time and in a place where such a thing could get a person killed, without much consequence. I had to talk a certain way, walk a certain way, be a certain way. I had to fit in. I perfected the act, until one day in Texas, senior year in college, when the lie was ripped away and the truth spilled out like the bloody entrails of a butchered animal.

I had to face a new reality. I had to deal with it. I had to survive those walks across campus where it seemed everyone found joy in shouting out words like "faggot" and "cocksucker" and "queer," perverting the beauty of their colloquial speech. It was a small school in a small town and everyone was in on the game.

Then one Friday night, I had to fight it.

A fraternity brother, Greg, came to my apartment half drunk and full of rage. He pounded on my door, screaming those words I heard every day. I could hear some of the other guys at the bottom of the stairs. "Damn, boy, give it a rest" or "you're gonna have the cops here, let's git outta here" and "what the hell's wrong with you, man, the girls are waitin' fir us."

I'd had enough. I was cornered, there was no other door. I couldn't run if I wanted to, but I didn't want to, not this time, not ever again. I opened the door, and he rushed in. He must have thought being gay made me smaller or weaker. It made me scared, yes, but that night, scared made me dangerous.

He came at me, eyes bloodshot from chugging cheap beer. Greg always drank before he drank. I fell back to buy some space, then grabbed his shirt and swung him around, intent on shoving him back out the front door, ready to throw punches. He was heavier than I expected. Instead of flinging him back the way he came, I sent him through the bank of windows set low in the wall next to the door.

He crashed through and landed on the porch. I heard a familiar voice shout "Holy shit!"

I stepped onto the front porch, looked down to the parking lot, glaring at the three below me. All of them dropped their "shit eatin' grins" in a hurry.

I looked back at my former friend, trying to extract himself from a glittering field of shattered glass, blood already flowing down his face in black-red rivers. My first impulse was to tell him I was sorry, to rush inside and grab a towel to staunch the bleeding, find some way to roll back the clock, try somehow to make things right.

When he looked up at me I could see the force of his hatred rising, the pale blotches of his face turning red, framed by ribbons of blood. "You fuckin' faggot!" he screamed, and started to rise.

His words purged that place in me that housed my empathy.

I was six foot two, and two hundred pounds of well honed muscle, with adrenalin and sobriety on my side. I grabbed him by his shirt again, pulled him the rest of the way to his feet, and flung him down the stairs.

I hadn't noticed the two guys rushing up, almost at my landing, until I released Greg to the open air. The ascending and descending forces collided, neutralizing one other. They fell back, none the worse for wear.

It could have ended there. They tried to pull Greg away, to end the mayhem. The neighbors would put up with a lot, especially when it came to me, but screams and shattering glass crossed the line. Greg shook them off, shoved them away, then turned to look up at me. Before he could speak, I started down the stairs.

All my life, even before that night and ever since, I have experienced profound states of calm in the most dire of circumstances. A car accident, a boat sinking beneath me, a gun pointed at my face, all of these things, and more, had already happened to me before that Friday night. Such situations, when most panic, bring me to an intense mental focus and physical calm. Some special cells in my brain take over and say, "You got this, let's go."

When this has happened, people have said I looked different, like another person, like no one they've ever seen before, someone that frightened them. Only years later did I learn it had a name - dissociation.

In the case of Greg, my first two steps toward him brought him to a halt and silenced his voice.

I didn't stop.

He step backwards and slipped on his own blood. He stumbled down to the shared landing between the two second-floor apartments, and fell to his knees, leaving another puddle of himself on the concrete surface.

I kept going.

He couldn't get to his feet, instead he grabbed the next step below him and pulled himself lower, away from me. The two who had abandoned him on the staircase came back. They grabbed him by the armpits and dragged him the rest of the way to the parking lot.

I maintained my deliberate pace.

The four of them backed away, all now speechless, until finally the one I knew wanted least of all to be there said "awright, dammit, awright, it's a 'nuff already."

Then I stopped. His voice grabbed my attention, then his eyes held it.

In a flash I relived the times we'd spent together, Mark and I. The football games, the parties, the booze, and of course that one particular night, after the party died down, our lives coming together in a fearful embrace that grew into something more. Something I thought would last forever.

Until I walked into his room one afternoon, using the front door key he'd given me almost as an afterthought. I knew the man he was with that day, but even if I hadn't, my heart was just as broken. The image of the two of them together, burned into my memory. I made my threats, and he made his, though mine were empty and his became my new reality, placing us on the path we were all now walking.

I suppose there's a fine line between powerful love and raging hate, and I'd found the way to push him, and everyone else it seemed, across that line. He told a few friends, and in a few day's time my secret life became an open book, a story to be told and spread with whispered voices in the halls and courtyards and ballfields of higher education.

I didn't know it then, but though he seemed safe behind his accusations and condemnations, his world was growing smaller and darker than it had ever been. Hindsight educates my understanding of him in a way the experience couldn't. All I knew then was betrayal, and the pain that came with it.

I looked into those eyes I'd awakened to so many

mornings, mere months since the last time, and felt it all again. I had to look away from him, to hold back my tears.

I scanned their faces, took note of Greg's fear, then returned to those piercing blue eyes that crushed my soul. When I saw the look on Mark's face, with no hint of sadness or regret, I didn't feel like crying after all.

"Forget I exist," I said, forcing as much disgust into my voice as my throat could carry, "I've already forgotten you."

I turned away and headed back up the stairs as the wailing sirens grew closer. I climbed up to my porch and sat on the edge, my legs draped over the top steps.

They piled Greg into the backseat of Mark's car and before he got in, Mark looked up at me. His face never changed, even as he raised his right hand and shoved his middle finger into the air, a performative act for everyone peeking out through their curtains to witness. I laughed at the impotence of it. He responded by getting in the driver's seat and slamming the door behind him.

I watched the life I'd known drive away, taillights rushing into the darkness, until the space around me filled with flashing blues and reds, sounds of brakes screeching to a sudden halt.

Four cars, eight officers in all. I guess someone convinced them it was necessary, or maybe they were just bored cops working in a small town. They held a little confab below me, then one of them made his way up the steps, scanning with his flashlight, trying not to step in any evidence.

I knew him and he knew me. I'd done a month of nightly ride-alongs with him as part of my criminal justice curriculum. "Hello Tom," I said. It'd been a while, but I knew we were still on a first-name basis, "how ya doin'?"

"I might ask you the same question," he said, "you wanna tell me what happened?"

"Not really."

"Any of this blood belong to you?"

"Nope."

"You wanna file a report?"

He was standing with his eyes level to mine, just a few feet away. I looked down at the gaggle of officers in the parking lot, all of them with a hand on a hip.

"No," I said. My voice was calm, my heart beat slow and steady, I felt lighter than I had in years.

"This gonna be a regular thing, ya think?"

"That's not up to me."

"No, I guess not," he said.

With a look down and a nod of his head, everyone but his partner returned to their cars and drove away, lights blinking out as they went. When they were gone, he leaned in and stared into my eyes. I returned his stare. "Buddy," he said, knowing I liked it when he called me that, "you know we can't protect you. There's just not…"

"Did I ask you to?"

"It's my job…"

"And you can't do it."

"I'm not your enemy…"

"Yes," I replied, cool as a Hill Country winter, "you are."

He pulled back and his voice rose an octave when he asked "How so?"

"The truth used to be my enemy. Now it's the lie. You're part of the lie."

He raised his palms up, "What do you want me to do?"

"Nothing."

We looked at each other until he shook his head and let out a sharp exhale that sounded like defeat.

"You sure you wanna stick it out here?"

"I've got three months, then I'm done, nobody's taking that from me."

"Might be easier for ya back in Georgia."

"Here, there, what's the difference?"

I looked over my shoulder at my ruined window, then down the stairs at the blood already drying on the steps.

"Besides," I said, "I think I made my point."

"You think this is gonna be the last of it?"

"Yes," I said, and believed it, "it's a small town, news travels fast."

After that night, I moved through the world like a boulder in a stream, life rushing around me as I waited out the weeks. Some still shouted their hate when I walked across campus, while a few made attempts at eye contact, flashing fervent smiles filled with sadness.

None of it mattered.

I was alone, an outcast in a world filled with lies.

But I wasn't afraid anymore.

A Time to Dance

My feet ached and my legs burned like fire. Hanging over the edge of a thousand-foot drop really fucked with my senses. I suppose I should explain how I ended up hanging by my wrists so high up. If I'm being honest, it had to do with all the people I killed. They deserved it, but not everyone saw it that way. I don't give a damn. Everywhere I went, somebody managed to get on my list.

The voices started out as just voices. Then they showed up in my apartment. Thin fuzzy gray things that oozed out of the walls and did this funky dance, all twisty and gray-black foamy puffs of nothing gyrating away in front of me until I sat up and took notice. After that, every time they showed up I knew what they wanted. More people dead.

I fought like hell the first few times, I think. I don't remember. I know one night, it was morning actually, but still night, I just accepted they owned me. There was no reasoning with them. Then I killed whoever they told me to kill. That's what they wanted me to do, so I did it.

One day it was a crotchety old man who drove too slow and flipped off everyone who honked at him, including me. Big mistake. Another time, it was this suburban douchebag with his fat ass wrapped in skinny jeans he stole from his gay brother-in-law while they vacationed at their lake house. He couldn't be bothered to make his kids shut up and settle down at the burger joint. He just let 'em raise holy hell and drive everybody nuts. Those little turds sealed his fate when one of 'em crashed into my table and spilled my beer.

Then there was this cute young princess who wouldn't stop yammering away on their phone in the checkout line at the grocery store, so damn rude. They never held up a line again.

My favorite was the snot-nosed punk from the private school down the street. That dumbass took a job at my neighborhood liquor store and couldn't be bothered to say 'thank you' when I paid for my case of vodka. I taught him some lessons. He reminded me of Lenny, if Lenny had clear skin and a pretty haircut.

It went on like that for years, maybe months. Time wasn't much to me, just a slow drag from point a to point b with a bunch of shit to do in-between. I think they thought I could get rid of all the rude, mean, nasty, condescending, dismissive, arrogant people in the world. That's a tall order for one guy. If Lenny hadn't left, he could have helped. Or maybe he would have ended up on the list. Hard to say.

They didn't like it if I let anyone get away, so I got better at it and eventually the TV was talking about a serial killer, one of the worst ever, but the TV didn't know it was me, it just knew it was somebody. Every channel had their own name for me, each of them tried to corner the market on the story. I got sick of hearing it, so I killed the TV, problem solved.

Then the cadre started to pay me visits. I knew what they were because they looked like those asshats from the military school the judge sent me to when I was a kid. Jail would have been better, at least there you can hit back. Want to make a horror movie? Follow a 12 year old around a military academy filled with psychopaths and pedophiles for a year, that shit will keep you up at night.

The cadre didn't ooze out of the walls like the fuzzy gray things and they damn sure didn't dance. I'd go to sleep and they would show up, all of them together, wearing their black and red regalia with their shiny gold faceplates. They looked liked Hell's Best Marching Band and when I said so they laughed and told me they didn't have anything to do with the music, that was a different department. I never did see their faces. I could hear them just fine, even through all that metal, which was weird at first but like everything else I got used to it.

They claimed me as their hero, said I had passed all the tests but one. I didn't know I was taking tests but I was sure happy to learn I'd been passing them. Hadn't passed a test since college, as far as I knew, not until the cadre showed up and told me I was their star pupil.

I liked college. Drink, smoke dope, have sex, me and Lenny never got tired of it. Guess that's why we dropped out, or they kicked us out, or maybe we just stopped going, I don't know. That was a long time ago.

Finding a job was a hell of a reality check. Lenny worked days, I worked nights, we never saw each other. I'm not even sure when he left. I came home after my overnight shift cleaning taxis and he was gone, along with almost everything in the apartment. Could have been a day, could have been a year, who gives a fuck? He was gone.

Cleaning taxis was a shit job, the lost wallets barely made up for the giz and bubblegum people smeared all over the back seat. You wouldn't believe what people get up to in those cars. It would make your skin crawl, if you had to clean it up. I got used to it.

My grandad finally died and left me a little something. That wheezy old fart never liked me and I don't know why he left me his money. Guess it was pity, or maybe I was the only one who would sit in a room with him. He stank of cheap cigars and piss and dirty diapers and never opened a window, not even on nice days. Maybe he wanted me to take care of all those cats he kept locked up with him. That was easy, I just left the door open. One more problem solved. I didn't give a shit they ate his face off, but the EMTs didn't take it well.

Anyway, I quit that job and focused on the task at hand. Guess that's why I started passing the tests, all but the last one. I got real busy after that, my list grew like the trash piles in the alley between my building and the burned out warehouse next door.

The last test was the best test, the cadre said, and if I could pass it I could take things to the next level, wherever that was. They told me I'd be happy there, could live like a king or even a god, and I guess that was good enough for me. If I could pass this last one, they told me, I could be rid of their fuzzy gray intermediaries. That sounded nice too.

All the killing was wearing me out, I almost never slept, which is why the cadre showed up whenever I did mange to catch some shuteye. They said they had to strike while the iron was hot, which made sense to me.

We went together up to the roof of my building. I didn't know where the roof was before then, I thought it was a lot lower. My building must have kept growing after I moved in, which is an odd thing to consider but it must have happened because it took a long time to get there and it was a long way down when I stepped to the edge.

"This is it," all of them said, "third time's the charm." I didn't recall a first or second time, but that didn't surprise me. My head was filled with gaps and dark spaces I'd given up trying to fathom. I didn't know what day it was most of the time, and I didn't much care. All of them laughed together when I had that thought. I sometimes forgot they could read my mind. I didn't think it was funny, but that didn't stop them from laughing.

I looked down and my city street had turned into a canyon, a dark black ribbon of river flowing through the middle and a big patch of sandy shore directly below me. Strange I could see so clearly so far down, but there it was.

Then they hung me out over the edge.

My feet ached and my legs burned. I never liked heights because my body didn't like heights. I couldn't even look at a picture of a height without that throbbing pain and burning sensation clawing at me, pulsing up through the soles of my feet and wrapping itself around my calves, squeezing and squeezing like it was trying to push my legs away from danger, all the blood jamming up at me all at once, burning all the way. People sitting on ledges, construction workers on skyscrapers, some dude about to jump out of an airplane. I couldn't look at any of it without that pain, that burning.

If you said height was the only thing I was afraid of you'd be spot on. I guess that's why they chose the roof for the final test.

I was dangling over a canyon 1000 feet deep. How it got there, I'll never know. The street was gone, the buildings were gone, everything was grey stone cliffs, burnt umber sky, yellow sand, black river.

My feet ached and my legs burned and I knew this was my last chance to pass the test.

"I can do it," I said, not entirely certain I could.

They laughed together again, and how they managed to all laugh the exact same way at the exact same time, well that's yet another mystery I'm not gonna solve, "You say that every time," all of them replied.   "I can do it, I swear!"

"You better hope so, this is your last chance."

Last chance. Last chance or what? Then it hit me.   I had to pass this test or things were never gonna change. I would go on forever, a ghost haunting the city. I would have to keep killing until I died of old age. It wasn't an entirely unappealing option. I was good at it. But I was getting tired of the fuzzy gray things always showing up like that, giving me orders, and the cadre, never letting me sleep.

This was my chance. I could move on, start some new phase of this little operation they'd spun up for me. I knew what had to happen next. I knew how to pass the test. The cadre always loved it when I swore at them, so I tried that little trick again.

"Fuck you, let me go!"

"Look at your hands. You're holding onto us."

They were right.

That was the trick. They didn't have to let go, I did. I could feel their flesh beneath mine, like rough stone scraping at my skin. I could see my fingernails bleeding from the white-knuckle grip, my palms shredding against their rough stony bones. Behind those shiny metal masks I was sure they were all smiling at me, certain I was about to fail again.

Not this time. I smiled back at them.

"Fuck you," I said again, just for fun, then I let go.

My feet ached and my legs burned and my heart pounded like one of those drums they use in an orchestra, the one that sounds like thunder, or bombs, or a cannon.

I fell some more until I wasn't falling, then stopped so quick I hardly noticed. Everything was quiet and dark for a while. Then it wasn't. Someone was laughing. Not the cadre's laughter, this was different. A softer sound, with the hint of a hiss and a bit of crackle, with a resonant rumble running beneath it.

I didn't open my eyes right away. I felt the gritty grains beneath my back, a hot breeze wafted over my face. I gripped the sandy soil with my fists, like a toddler squeezing a big fat finger just for the feel of it.

The laughter again, closer, not approaching but drifting

somewhere behind me, pulling me into the place I'd landed. I sat up. I opened my eyes.

The canyon walls were gone. The fuzzy grays were gone. The cadre were gone. Everything was burnt umber sky boiling over the horizon and rolling above the sand and the river and me, so close I tried to touch it.

I felt a rapturous blast of heat at my back, turned to look and saw the black ribbon of river carrying a tall spinning spire of fire twisting away over the middle of the current. The fire danced and twirled and laughed, maybe at me, maybe not. Maybe it liked being fire and laughed at everything.

My head itched and my feet tingled and my legs began to twist and crack and shape into something bizarre yet familiar, like something from a book I'd read back when I still cared about books. It was a thick one bound in leather and one time my mother slammed it against my wrist to crush what she called a preacher's wart. I think it worked, the lump went away and my hand still managed to do what it was meant to do.

I smiled when I felt the horns growing from my skull, then marveled at their beauty and symmetry as they curved and twisted up and the pointy tips curled in toward each other. I couldn't help but laugh.

The fire heard me. It reached out a flickering red-orange appendage and whipped its tip a few times, seducing me with light and heat and motion, a tongue begging for a kiss, or possibly something else.

I rose and stood on black cloven hooves where once my feet had been. Ankles, knees and hips clad in oily fur and bending in directions I didn't know they could go, all opposite of where they'd once been.

I stumbled at first, then found my balance and stepped onto the river, walked over the flow, and danced with the fire, laughing and laughing and laughing, until all the world was fire and motion and deep rumbling throat noises wrapped up in crackles and hisses and pops.

I'd never danced before, but now found I couldn't stop, not if I wanted to. But my feet didn't ache and my legs didn't burn.

It was time to dance, and I had a sense from then on, it always would be.

Dust and Memories

It started, as tragedy often does, with a small thing, a little tremble in his hand. He dismissed it as a minor injury, a strain or pull from working too hard in the garden. It came and went, then it came and never left. By the time he went to the doctor, he was struggling to play his cello. By the time we had a diagnosis, his instrument was gathering dust in its stand in the sunroom where he practiced, and entertained our frequent guests. Frequent, until we chose to share his prognosis. Our many acquaintances all but disappeared after the surgery.

We believed it when they told us the operation would buy us more time. What we didn't expect was for Mitch to be an invalid, trapped in a hospital bed in our dining room - the bedroom was too small - unable to speak, barely able to move, in need of constant care. The surgery bought us six months, at a terrible cost. He couldn't say it, but I knew he regretted the decision. It would have been better to let the lesions on his brain do their worst and have it over with, months of clarity, days of pain, the end.

A friend who lived down the street, Ethan, never stopped coming to visit while Mitch was still alive. In his late twenties, not many years younger than Mitch, we both liked him from the moment we met him at a dinner party two years before Mitch's hand began to shake. Mitch loved to play for him. Ethan confessed he'd wanted to learn the cello when he was in elementary school, but his parents refused, claiming the instrument was too large for a third-grader to haul around. It wasn't, of course, Mitch started younger. But it wasn't cheap and neither were lessons, and at the time Ethan's father had yet to attain his wealth. Ethan ended up with a trumpet and a tyrant for a teacher. His musical career was over before it started, by high school he'd turned his attention to sports, and other pursuits. But he never lost his love for music and would spend as much time listening to Mitch as Mitch was willing to spend playing. Mitch would play and stop now and again to tell stories of his travels with his quartet, or his time as first chair in the orchestra.

Mitch would play, I would cook, and after dinner Ethan would rifle through our record collection, playing album after album until either Mitch or I fell asleep on the sofa. As Mitch lost control of his hands, Ethan became a kind of conductor, selecting music to accompany our evenings and afternoons together, always seeking to orchestrate a brighter mood, or perhaps a more gentle passing. In retrospect, it's hard for me to say which. It seems to me now that he knew more than I realized, or perhaps he simply understood things from a different perspective. His father had been dead for years. Cancer had taken a vicious toll on Ethan's family, first it killed his father, then it came for him, and finally for his mother. Though the two of them survived, that sort of history leaves a mark. For Ethan, I suspect, it permanently altered the frame through which he viewed the world.

On one of his last visits, Ethan brought a record he'd found at a second-hand store in Charlottesville, Virginia. A collection of string quartets by Bartók, performed by Emerson String Quartet. "They won a grammy for this album," he said, "I didn't know you could win a grammy for classical."

Mitch managed something akin to a laugh. By then he'd regained some movement, and the ability to vocalize, though proper speech would never return. Ethan, like me, knew Mitch was still there, trapped within a body that no longer followed his mind's commands. I'd moved the stereo into the dining room when the hospital bed arrived. I would leave it playing softly on Mitch's favorite station, NPR, each night in hopes it would help him sleep. I watched as Ethan cleaned the record before placing it on the turntable, then I turned my attention to our meal.

From the kitchen I heard Ethan's running commentary. "This one sounds like the opening scene of a horror movie." I imagined Mitch's smile, his inner laughter. "This one's downright jaunty," Ethan said, amusing himself again. Then a somber piece began and the commentary stopped. When Ethan's silence persisted, I went to investigate. I found him seated next to the bed, his head resting on the edge by Mitch's side, holding Mitch's hand. Mitch had placed his free hand on the back of Ethan's neck. They were both crying.

Mitch saw me and his eyes said all I needed. I left them to their moment. Over dinner Ethan told me what he had told Mitch. He was leaving at the end of the month. He'd taken a job in Atlanta, an opportunity he couldn't turn down. "It's time to start acting my age," he said, "the pay is awesome, the benefits are great, there's lots of room to grow."

"You got your degree for a reason," I told him.

"I'll come back as often as I can. I need some time to get settled, still haven't found a place, it's complicated. I won't have parking privileges for the first sixty days. Dumbass rule, but what can you do?"

"You can stay at Mitch's condo. You can walk to the subway, you won't have to drive to work."

Mitch had achieved a measure of fame for his artistry. He owned a small condo in a grand old building on The Prado, a park-like Atlanta street connecting the botanical gardens to Symphony Hall, known for its mansions and manicured lawns. The location had enabled Mitch to walk to work during the season, when he wasn't traveling.

It would be an elegant stepping stone for Ethan. Of course he accepted, and I was grateful he did. A home should never sit empty too long.

"Thank you George," he said after dinner, then hugged me before walking down the street into the darkness.

Two days later Mitch died in his sleep. The time between his death and his funeral was lost to me, nothing more than slow movement through a dense fog. The day after the service, Mitch's family came to the house and started removing the things they decided to claim.

I had purchased our house, a 1920's brick bungalow on an enormous lot in the heart of old Athens, a high brick wall surrounding us to keep out the world, a compact barn to house the tools of my trade as an arborist. The property was cheap, it needed a complete overhaul, and it cost the bulk of my life savings once the final bill was tallied. I was happy to bear that cost. We filled the house with old furniture, art, ceramics, and photographs from our life together. We scavenged estate sales, swap meets, picked out at least one item from every antique store we ever visited, and there were many. I knew where every piece was purchased, and when. I knew the weather and the time of day and our moods at the moment of each acquisition.

Mitch had bequeathed a few items to his multitudinous siblings and his parents, which they took as license to abscond with whatever they wanted. They never accepted us, or perhaps me, but that didn't prevent them from appreciating our taste. I didn't have the energy to stop them, or maybe I lacked the interest. My hands were full of lawyers and reappearing friends. Once the items left the house, they took with them the memories they held, the stories they told of our time together, all lost on their new owners.

When Ethan saw what they had done, how much they had taken, he flew into an uncharacteristic rage. "How could they," he cried, "fucking animals!"

"I'll be fine without them," I said, "I wish they'd left the dining room set, now that the bed is gone I was going to bring it back in from the barn. Not sure who spotted it out there but they had it loaded and gone before I knew they'd found it."

Ethan balled his fists, his face crimson red, his eyes filled with tears. The previous six months had left me empty, drained of any feeling. I had no time for tears, no energy for anger. "You need to let it go," I said, "I have."

He left without responding then returned twenty minutes later, pulling his old pickup through the gate next to the barn. He brought the chairs in first, then I helped with the table and leaf.

"It's not an antique," he said, "but it's a fine table. My mother bought it years ago, when she had a bigger house. My brother had it for a while, the damage is from him, not me. Use it as long as you want, you know I won't need it."

He was right, it was a fine table. Solid oak with veneer inlay, beautifully turned legs, and four handsome chairs, all made by hand in North Carolina. I was familiar with the maker. I knew quality when I saw it, and I knew neglect as well. But it wasn't beyond saving, and I was grateful for the loan. We set it up with the leaf in place and I made lunch so we could dine at it together.

While Mitch's family had taken much, they'd left all of his clothes. I soon shed the weight I'd gained during his illness, then began to wear his things. They looked like him, smelled like him, felt to me as he once felt, fine cloth under the rub of a calloused hand. When winter set in I pulled a pair of his flannel-lined jeans from a box in the attic and wore them on the colder days. I knew the more I did this, the less life they would have, but they were all I had left of him and I would risk their loss to have him close again, to feel him against my skin. To remember him.

I spent my evenings, drink in hand, staring at his cello in the corner, willing it to bring forth music again. Some nights, in the small hours, I could hear his music wafting through the air as my eyes fluttered down, fighting against sleep. I would dream of him. I began to long for sleep, for the dream, to embrace the chance to see him without the pain and the grief. I learned to live in the dream, it was all that kept me in the world. I sold my business when the strain of the work no longer comforted me. My life became the counting of days in the dim light of an empty house, the collecting of dust, and the fading of memories.

As winter receded and spring approached, I ventured back into the attic to seek out a light coat I knew Mitch had stowed away with other items suited to the season. The single bare bulb cast spare light, I needed a flashlight for a proper search. It was then I found the two large moving boxes tucked away in a darkened corner. They had not been there long enough to become encrusted in grime like everything else in the attic.

The boxes were taped shut and marked "Fragile." I knew the handwriting belonged to Mitch. I abandoned my search for the jacket and carried the boxes to the more comfortable space of my living room. I took a knife from the kitchen and carefully unsealed the first box. When I saw the contents, my heart stopped for a moment, then began to race, pounding away in my chest as if it wished to burst out and run free.

I lifted the first frame from the box, a picture of me from our anniversary trip to Napa. I remembered how we started wine tastings so early we were mostly drunk by lunch, amusing the driver we'd hired to haul us around the valley. I set it aside and lifted the second frame out. A photo of Mitch and me in Paris, taken by a fellow tourist. At the time, I half expected the man who took it to run off with the camera, but I knew Mitch would chase him down if he did. The memory, the absurdity of my fear, made me smile. I lingered over it, then stood and placed one photo on the mantle, and hung the other on a leftover hook by the front window. Then there was a picture of Mitch standing alone in front of a low wall at the zoo. Behind him an elephant was taking a dump. "I love this one," I said aloud, "you hated the zoo and went with me anyway. That's love."

I emptied the box, photos from every trip we'd ever taken, a few from weddings we'd attended, one of my nephew on the day he was born. I gave each its rightful place, then returned to the sofa to open the second box, the heavier of the two.

More photos, some in need of frames, were stacked on top. I set these aside in favor of the contents below, a collection of figurines, ceramics, and other small art objects.

The first object was a little carved Buddha from our trip to an antique show south of Atlanta a few weeks after we moved into the house. Mitch was convinced it was ivory. He wouldn't hear it when I told him it was bone. We fought about it all the way home, such a long ride. When he figured out I was right he wouldn't stop apologizing. Then I apologized, then him again. We were such a mess back then. But it taught us an important lesson, namely that make-up sex is the best. I couldn't help but laugh at the thought.

I placed the figure on a shelf next to the fireplace, then took each of the remaining items out, carefully unwrapping them, holding them, reliving their stories, before giving each a home.

Only after the last items were removed did I discover the box within the box.

It was a nondescript cardboard flat, a few inches high, the dimensions of a large book. It was light as a feather and at first I thought it might be empty. It was taped shut and I again recognized Mitch's elegant script flowing along one edge.

'Ethan - Summer - 2016'

It was the summer we learned of Mitch's death sentence. I thought at first it was a gift for Ethan that we had somehow forgotten or overlooked. We celebrated his birthday with him each May, but I had no recollection of such a box.

It was taped shut much the same as the gift-wrapped presents Mitch gave me each Christmas, copious amounts of paper and tape designed to withstand the apocalypse. I smiled again, knowing his hands had done their usual work.

The box contained one thing, a folder made of thick blue paper. I pulled it out and set the box aside. More of Mitch's writing greeted me on the front of the folder.

'For George, My Love'

I placed the folder on the coffee table and opened it, my heart pounding, hands trembling, fear and longing colliding. Inside, a single color photo, enlarged.

It was a picture of Ethan wading knee deep in the shoals downstream from the falls on a remote part of Panther Creek. I knew the place well, Mitch and I had gone camping there many times over the years, before we could afford more exotic trips. Ethan was naked, the sun was low, the sky a mix of blazing orange and clear blue, the water sparkled with light, his skin bathed in gold. It was a glorious sight, a beautiful menagerie of forest, stone and river, of light, and sun-kissed flesh.

I didn't know who took the picture, only that it wasn't taken by me. I flipped the image over, hoping the photographer had the courtesy to sign their name. What I found was a letter from Mitch, exquisite in its brevity.

My Dearest George,

By now I am gone, but I will carry this moment with me forever, because it was meant for you. He is afraid to tell you he loves you, and you are probably afraid to hear it. But your life is not over, you deserve to be happy and to make some new memories. I expect to hear all about it when I see you again, in the life after this.

All My Love,

Mitch

I turned the image over and stared. I felt the tears begin to flow, a dam of pain collapsing under a burden held back too long. I let go, stopped trying, gave my grief free rein. I did not return to myself until the sun was setting beyond the trees, and shadows had overtaken the house. Then I slept, there on the sofa. This time my dreams left me alone.

I woke before dawn and looked out at the garden, saw the last of Orion twinkling in the sky, chased away by the pre-dawn light. A cardinal poked its red crest out from the rose bush overcrowding the patio, then ducked back into its nest. I heard a neighbor's car come to life, the nurse next door leaving for their shift. The world was turning, life went on.

I made a pot of coffee, and sat sipping it at the table Ethan had left for me. At 6:00am, I dialed his number.

"Georgie," he said, "what's going on? Everything all right?"

"Did I wake you?"

"No, I'm up. I was about to go for a run. Is something wrong?"

"Nothing's wrong. Do you have time to talk?"

"For you, always. You sound tired Georgie, what's…"

"Will you tell me about the picture, the one of you, at the river…I found it in the attic."

There was a long silence, then a soft exhale. I imagined I could hear him smile.

"I was wondering what happened to that. Mitch took it,

what a day. I'll tell you the story, I've been saving it. It's a good one. I think you're gonna love it."

"I bet I will, I'm sure you made some memories."

"It's the weekend, what say I drive out and we talk about it."

"I'd like that. Should I plan lunch or dinner?"

"How about both? George, be honest with me, are you sure you're all right?"

"Yeah, I am. I'm better than all right. I think I'm good. Or I will be. I'm better anyway."

"It's good to hear your voice, I've been hoping for a call like this."

"Me too, Ethan, me too. See ya soon."

We ended the call and I looked around, seeing clearly for the first time how I'd let the house go. I went to the kitchen, grabbed some damp towels, and got to work, clearing away the dust and cobwebs and remnants of a time I was, at last, ready to forget, surrounded once again by the better moments of a life I would always remember.

Ghosts of Winter

One need not live on Boston's South Shore for long to become familiar with the sound of trees dying. The soil is rich, but the most abundant crop here is rocks, granite remnants of the glacial parade that formed the land. We live nestled against a wetland, a place we would call a swamp in the South. Trees fall with such regularity, they go largely unnoticed. But gale force winds crack them apart mid-trunk, with a sound that travels far and heralds the following thump of impact surrounded by the rushing crackle and snap of the neighbors the tree takes down with it.

Born in the Gulf of Mexico, the storm ravaged the Florida peninsula. It spent its early strength of wind and water in the dark of night, then boiled over the Atlantic. It regrouped and tormented the eastern seaboard before settling over New England with high winds, but little by way of precipitation, until it collided with the force of a colder airmass descending from the Arctic.

The wind howled and tore at the forest, trees formed piles on the earth like a giant game of pick-up-sticks. The electricity lasted mere hours, internet and cell service died soon after, our generator no cure for a lack of connectivity. Four days we lived on fumes and frustration. It seemed a lifetime, then it was over. The lights came back, then everything else followed the next day, including a deluge, soaking the Christmas Holiday and dampening our spirits yet further.

The rain ended during the fifth night and we awoke to warmer temperatures and dense fog. The world was grey and black, pale light and shallow shadows. We were not experiencing the snow-laden winter we'd been promised, but we spent our evenings in front of the fireplace nonetheless, as much to drive away the damp and the dark as to keep ourselves a little warmer.

The stark beauty of the fog drew us out into the world. We drove along the narrow winding roads to Scituate, bypassing the town center, curving around it to make our way to the lighthouse overlooking the breakwater at the outer edge of the harbor. The pleasure boats had been pulled from the water weeks earlier. They stood resolute against the weather, swaddled in bright white vinyl, gathered like ghosts of the winter sea, standing stark against the battleship sky.

The sea was calm and rolled gently against the massive stone blocks of the breakwater. Its arms stretched out to embrace the waves, guarding homes and boats and businesses within. But evidence of the previous fury was abundant. Mangled lobster pots the most visible victims of the storm's rage, crumpled and jammed between the rocks. They would be left where they landed to rust and decay, never again to earn their keep.

A metal tower capped with lights stood at the distant end of the outermost line, a guide to any vessels seeking refuge in the harbor. I stood with the landmark lighthouse behind me and watched the tower lights pulse red, until others joined them. Bright white flashes breached the fog beyond the tower. My partner retreated to the comfort of the car while I kept watch on the approaching lights.

A fishing boat formed in the fog, its lights the only sign of life. No hands worked the deck, no movement inside. Rigging aloft, nets stowed on deck, it slipped into the mouth of the harbor, a soundless apparition making steady way. I thought it was a ghost, like its kin lining the shore, until it turned inside the breakwater, on an unexpected heading toward the empty moorings of the yacht club. There was nothing for it there, and it altered course again, still not aiming for the commercial center of the harbor. I could not fathom its odd path. But there are more things I do not know about the sea and the ships that work it than I will ever learn.

Once the ship was lost to the mist of the inner harbor, I returned to the car with its warm air and heated seats. We drove too-fast back to our house, but sunset beat us all the same. I lit a fire and we tucked in for the evening, TV news blathering away while we buried ourselves in our devices. News of our town breached my indifference. A couple, elderly, a mile from us, had died. Carbon monoxide poisoning. Their generator killed them, days before they were discovered.

Despite being outside, our own generator had cut out several times due to the buildup of this deadly gas. The sensor so delicate, a change in the wind could set it off, shutting down our power. Older generators lacked the technology we took for granted and occasionally cursed. It was a nuisance, but we were alive, and our neighbors, if you could call them that, were not.

In this land of narrow roads and absent sidewalks, where live-and-let-live is the polite version of mind your own business, one does not learn the names or faces of those who live out of visual range. Four homes within sight of ours, and these are the only people we know. It is a stark contrast to life in the suburbs of Atlanta, where we knew everyone who wanted to be known.

The fire died down and I rose to toss more captured carbon

into the flames. We burn wood, fuel from felled trees which would otherwise go to waste. Cheaper than the oil, the warmth more immediate. We do not burn pine, of course. It would stink and fill the chimney with creosote, another way for the winter to kill, a house burning while its occupants slumber.

While the dog snored, I refilled my glass then slumped back into my armchair. For the 'nth' time since returning to New England I ask myself, 'What am I doing here?' and I reply, 'Adapting.' I am adapting, where before, two decades ago, I failed to see this part of the country for the alien and hostile place it is, one that does not welcome outsiders, any more than it welcomed my ancestors centuries before me. I refused then to accept that I had to force my life into it, and retreated, after two terrible winters, to the sunbelt from whence I came.

This time, there is no retreat. There is only this place and the life I can make in it, carve from it, squeeze out of it. I relish the effort. It reminds me I am alive. I have worked the land, tamed the forest, drained the weather into the wetlands, replaced the towering pines with a crop of green grass and flowering shrubs. I sit by the fire waiting for the warmth and color of spring, and the labor it will force upon me. I need the exercise. I've grown fat in the cold.

It is January, weeks of winter lie ahead and I wonder how they will turn. Have we been spared the worst this time around? How many ghosts before it's over?

The night hardly differs from the day, shrouded in fog created by two masses colliding in a colossal stalemate. The fire is glowing embers, the nagging noise of the television gone for another night. I drain my glass and drift away into the grey mist, wrapped in warmth and silence and my memories of brighter days.

In the morning if there is sun I will split more wood from

our pile and stack it neatly beside the fireplace, hopeful it will last between storms. While the work does warm me, twice in fact, there is no value in working in the rain, only soggy clothes and fuel that will not catch. In the morning, if there is sun, I will work outside and bend nature to my will once more. If not, I will be at my desk, working on words. I will adapt to whatever the day brings. It is winter's gift to me, time to be alone with my thoughts, time to write. The light and color and air of Spring and Summer always win the contest for my attention, drawing me away from my desk and keyboard and notebooks.

I have learned from the capricious nature of the weather in these parts that one must take advantage, when advantage is offered. For now, I stand still within the winter, gazing at a frigid sea, casting faint light into the darkness. But I am still here, I am still alive, and will be when this winter ends. Until then, I am content among the ghosts and the shadows and the fog. I have adapted.

The Not-Zombies Apocalypse

It took a while, but eventually we figured out killing the zombies was a bad idea. We lit upon that bit of logic right after we figured out killing infected people was a bad idea. It just made worse zombies.

We call them zombies but they're not zombies in the traditional sense. They're not reanimated corpses roaming the land ravenous for brains. Our zombies don't work that way, but we call them zombies because it's easy, everybody knows the word, and it's not like we're in some TV show where actors pretend to be people who have never heard of zombies. The word was available and sort of fit, so we used it.

In our not-zombies zombie apocalypse things are a lot different from any portrayal of same said situation in print or film.

We still have electricity, we still have TV (though it's all reruns at this point), people go to work, kids are being born, lives are being lived. But nowadays we have these flesh-eating maybe-immortals without functioning brains running around all over the place.

I'm exaggerating. They don't actually eat flesh, unless of course it's their only option.

It's true our zombies are prone to biting people. They get

hungry, so you can hardly blame them. It's not like they can walk into a Taco Bell and order a Nachos Bell Grande. Still, doesn't matter, a bite's a bite and it carries a ninety-nine percent chance of infection.

That's why we know killing infected people doesn't work, but putting masks on the zombies does. For the record, our zombies don't talk. How weird would that be?

It all started when some lab someplace let a virus loose, that virus mutated, people got infected, the infection spread, and next thing you know it's a global pandemic. Sound familiar?

Only this time the infected weren't dying. Their brains were dying, but their bodies got super-healthy. If they were obese they lost weight, if they were underweight they put on lean muscle mass, if they had cancer they were suddenly cancer free. The infected became paragons of health and fitness, without having to go to a gym or eat a sensible diet. The virus cures everything and it slows, in some cases reverses, the aging process.

The side effect of this miracle of modern misapplied science is a little thing the CDC dubbed "sudden generalized brain atrophy." In other words, infected people become exceptionally stupid, hence the zombie moniker.

But again, our zombies aren't dead and they show no signs of dying any time soon. On the flip side, if you kill somebody after they get bitten by one of these walking runway models, as a sort of preemptive strategy, that person does become a for-real flesh-eating, body-rotting, moan-and-groan zombie.

Nobody's figured out why this happens, but it happens and we've learned to live with it. As a society we figured out the best move was to stop killing these people and let them sort it out with their God, their families and the government.

What would you do? Keep poor Uncle Joey alive, to wander around in a perpetual stupor, always on guard against the possibility he might want to nibble on you from time to time? Believe it or not, a lot of people choose that option.

Especially since we've figured out what to do with the ever-increasing number of walking brain-dead. Turns out, even a tiny bit of functioning brain can be taught to do all kinds of useful things.

Like take out the garbage, mop the floor, or, and this seems to be one of the more popular tricks, walk the dog. Some would argue the dog is walking the zombie, but you say tomato, I say pickles, who cares who's right? It's the results that matter.

Our zombies like to walk, they never sit down, so whoever came up with the dog walking idea, kudos to them and thank you for sharing. But these activities burn calories and the last thing you want on your hands is a hangry zombie.

Sugar cubes to the rescue. Our zombies will do almost anything for a sugar cube. They're mad for the stuff. One thing you can say about our zombie apocalypse, it's been good for the refined sugar industry.

Plus, our zombies never get fat, never get diabetes, never get rotten teeth. The virus takes care of everything, all they need is for calories consumed to meet or exceed calories burned. It's a balancing act, yes, but you get used to it.

On the other hand, the plague has been a disaster for the entertainment industry. Before the apocalypse was in full swing, a lot of people scoffed at the idea that we were facing yet another pandemic. There was no way movie and TV production was going to get shut down again. Plus, what was left of the big theater chains fought a winning battle to remain open even as the virus was rapidly turning every actor, producer, director, best boy, grip and caterer in the business into a very healthy likely-to-live-forever-but-can't-even-dress-itself zombie.

Reruns rule the day.

It's not as bad as it sounds. There's a lot of comedy gold left in the "Golden Girls," and there's plenty of gas left in the "Deadpool" tank, so we manage. Even the theaters have seen an uptick in sales by bringing back the classics, like "Casablanca" and "Die Hard." That last one's a big draw every Christmas, but we buy our tickets early so we can get seats in the theater's acoustic sweet spot.

That's another good use for our zombies, standing in line. You see it all the time now, at theme parks, theaters, the DMV, anyplace there's a line, there's at least one zombie, usually a lot more, standing in it while their person - that's what we call someone who has a zombie in their life, 'their person' - is off grabbing a coffee, buying groceries, or just sitting in their car watching Netflix. There was a time when lines were often made up entirely of zombies, but that got really weird really fast, so most places have limits on the percentage of zombies that can stand in any given line.

By weird I mean, think about what happens when a zombie is next in line and their person is nowhere to be seen. What's it supposed to do? It can't speak, can't write, can't do much more than it's been trained to do - stand there and step forward when there's an empty space in front of it. This does not go over well with the less fortunate humans who lack a zombie of their own and have to stand in line. Plus, all it takes is one jerk with a pocket full of sugar cubes to cause a zombie stampede, at which point everyone has to corral their zombies and queue them up all over again, assuming no one got bitten. It's a mess, hence the rules.

This line-standing function, plus dog walking capabilities, is why Jesse and I decide we should have our own personal zombie. I know what you're thinking and no, you cannot buy a zombie. The very idea is, well, gross.

But what you can do is lease one, either from someone who

has an extra one walking around, which is a great way to dip your toe into the zombie pool, or via a pre-order from someone who's infected but hasn't yet lost their mind. An entire new business model has sprung to life around this idea - zombie brokers.

For Jesse and me, we didn't want the first option, it just seemed too impersonal. We wanted to know our zombie before it came to live with us, so we went the broker route.

It was a lot like making design selections for a new house. You went to a nice office, met with the company rep, told them what you were looking for, they asked a bunch of questions, made you sign a bunch of documents (including the one where you promise to never 'take advantage' of your zombie), and viola, you're pre-qualified for zombie companionship.

It works like this: someone gets infected and they have a certain number of days before their cognitive decline kicks into high gear. Their options are limited. Health insurance companies are utterly useless since there's no treatment, and life insurance is even more worthless because the person isn't going to die. The families of the infected get completely screwed. There's always the euthanasia option, but that involves dying only to become a reanimated corpse that has to be cremated… I mean, it's a nasty bit of business.

Instead, infected people, while they're still able to think, can opt to broker their services to the non-infected. Everything is on the up and up and only adults are allowed to make this choice. Most of those who do this seem to find a measure of peace in the fact their bodies will be put to good use and their families will get a nice payday.

This industry has saved a lot of families' futures.

Once we were pre-qualified for zombie companionship (never ever call it ownership - that is just wrong. You don't own your kids, do you?), Jesse and I spent a day meeting with our potential future zombie companions. We're gay, but we aren't bigots, so we met with both men and women. It was an interesting experience.

You could tell the newbies because they were usually hesitant about the whole process, not quite sure if they had made the right choice. The more experienced ones, those who had been in the system for a few days and hadn't gotten a contract yet, they always seemed to put a little more effort into the engagement.

Eventually we settled on a robust young man named Eric who'd been bitten in a zombie stampede at the DMV while trying to renew his driver's license. He claimed he wasn't gay, but felt like being in a gay household would be best for him, something about hating kids. He wouldn't know us from a cantaloupe by the time he moved in with us, so really, who cares? It gave him some measure of comfort, and who were we to question it? After all, we were going to be doing as much, maybe more, for him than he would for us.

Thankfully, while zombies can't manage to put their clothes on, the brokerage makes sure they're fully house-trained before delivery and they come with a special easy-on easy-off wardrobe.

We decide to name him Ken (of course we didn't tell him this). During our interview he told us his reason for the zombie companion option was that he hoped one day there would be a cure and he could go back to being a normal human again. It was such a cute bucket of naivety, we just had to have him.

Plus, he was one of the more affordable options. He didn't have a spouse or kids, and he didn't want to wait around forever to get chosen. He was eminently practical, another adorable trait.

We tapped our HELOC, handed over the cash, and waited for Ken's brain to fizzle. In the meantime, we introduced him to our dog, the neighbors, the local police, anybody we thought needed to know that this new zombie wandering the neighborhood was our zombie companion, and he should be left in peace to do our bidding. I don't know what Ken thought of all this, but he seemed to like meeting people while he still could. The dog loved him, and that's really the most important thing.

Now here we are, me and Jesse and Brody (the dog) and Ken, living the life. Ken is great with Brody, and Brody seems to like circling the block six or seven times with Ken in tow.

Ken is also great at vacuuming, though we had to move some of the furniture around because he kept crashing into it. And he's gotten good at taking out the garbage and recycling, so long as we bang on the trash can with a wooden spoon three times to let him know it's time to get to work. We're hoping he'll figure out how to do this without a prompt, but hey, at least I don't have to schlep the dumpsters down to the curb and back twice a week.

We tried to teach him how to boil water once, but you can imagine how that went. It took Jesse three hours to convince the ER doc we weren't abusing our zombie.

We mostly have our meals delivered, but the delivery services are having a tough time keeping their drivers - unemployment is at an all-time low so every now and then we have to go fetch our food ourselves. If only zombies could drive.

We get our allotment of sugar cubes delivered every week as well. There's a sugar shortage right now, but they say the supply chain will normalize soon. We get ours via a subscribe-and-save deal from you-know-where, but the success rate for delivery is about 50 percent these days. Until then we supplement Ken's diet with crickets (he will not eat cooked meat under any circumstance - go figure). They're a great source of protein and I swear Ken gets a kick out of eating them alive. I told Jesse I saw Ken smile once while he was eating his crickets, but he refused to believe it until I set up a camera to catch Ken in the act.

Things did get a little worrisome when Ken started laughing. Even Jesse couldn't deny it. We were watching "Golden Girls" for the umpteenth time and in one episode, the one where one of the gals tries to hide something from the others and fails and hilarity ensues, and out of nowhere Ken laughs right along with us.

It was a little creepy, if I'm being honest. I said zombies never sit down, and Ken is no different. We've trained him to hang out in the corner in the living room when we don't need him, which he does without complaint as long as he's not facing the wall and he's not hungry. We tried to get him to stand facing the wall, but he invariably turns around to face the TV. If we try to force the issue he starts making this horrible sad moaning-whining-teeth-grinding noise, a cross between whale song and fingernails on a chalkboard. We've learned to avoid upsetting him.

Our zombie broker said all of this is normal stuff for the Ken's of the world. He explained how zombies are just gonna do some stuff out of muscle memory or deep-seated connections to something in their past, or for who knows why, and it was really nothing to worry about, even if it does freak us out a little. We talked with other families who had a zombie in the house and most say something like "oh yeah, that happens all the time, don't sweat it."

We try not to sweat it, but now we can't watch TV without watching at least one episode of "Golden Girls" first. Ken won't shut up until we do, so we got smart and added the series to our 'regular recordings' list in our streaming app. Wherever we go, we always have an episode on an iPad close at hand in case we need it to appease Ken.

We feel lucky, on several fronts. Neither of us, Jesse or me, have gotten infected. We have this helpful, good looking young man around to do whatever chores we can teach him to do, and we feel like we brought Ken into our lives just in the nick of time since there's talk of a vaccine coming out soon, mere months away they say.

Just think what a vaccine will do to the price of our zombies, it'll go through the roof. Then again, a lot of people are saying there's no way in hell they'll take a new vaccine, which is fine by me and Jesse. We're thinking about adding a second zombie to our happy little family, so if people want to continue to risk infection, that's OK by us.

It's all about supply and demand after all. As long as there are stupid people in the world, there'll be a steady supply of zombie stupid along with them.

I think we'll name the next one Karen.

Penance

I was sober the day James returned to me, as I had been every day since the day after he left. It didn't matter to the world, but it mattered to him, and it finally mattered to me. I was where he wanted me to be, on our secret beach, with its view of our mooring in the harbor.

I never knew I could spend a year without him. Twelve months without running my fingers through his hair, without his lips pressed against mine, not so much as a graceful whisper of a touch.

It was my penance, and I did not pay it gladly, not at first.

As my health and head recovered there was a time filled with self-righteous disdain when I thought I'd move on and let him have his justified anger, tell him to stay out there, wherever he was, on the ocean we both loved.

Then my loneliness and regret took hold, stripped away my ego, and laid bare my shame. That was the moment I knew things had changed for me.

I never hurt him and he never hurt me, not in the traditional sense. But we both left our marks, mine perhaps more permanent against his innocence and naivety. He was young when we met, his joy for life stark against my cynicism. Early in our relationship he laughed at my jokes, filled with acid wit, until somewhere in the middle years he realized I'd stopped trying to be funny.

I didn't blame him when he left me, but I raged at him all the same. "How can you walk away," I screamed at the screen door slamming behind him. "Now, of all the times you could have left, how can you leave me now?" When he didn't look back, I gave up my last impotent rant, "I'll be stuck here all winter because of you."

A tiny village on the ocean is a beautiful place to spend a New England winter, unless you're struggling with sobriety. There's not a damn thing to do but eat away your feelings and drink away your remorse, not for me anyway.

The first night without him I expected my whole body to shake, feared my heart would shudder and quake and come to a complete stop. But my hands didn't shake, my heart didn't stop.

The shaking started after few nights without a drink or a toke or a line of blow to ease my imaginary pain. I had my moments of fear and self-doubt, wanted so often to walk down the sandy road to the liquor store and snatch up a bottle of wasted of money.

Instead I received everything the absence of all my vices could throw at me. I wanted to feel it, all of it. What good is sobriety if there's still nothing to feel?

I slept like shit the first night of my delirium, if you could call it sleep and if shit wakes up every so often to cry or scream or vomit.

I hadn't bothered to work for a long time, not a single word written or even thought about, so it didn't much matter. Each day I slid out of bed before dawn, had a microwaved breakfast, took a walk down to the harbor, then came home and napped on the sofa while the news of the world blurred away on the television.

One day I woke up, took some time to gather my thoughts yet again, this time much easier than the day before, then I allowed myself to miss him.

It went on that way for a month, perhaps longer. Days are meaningless when the sky never changes and the stars are seldom seen. Calendars pointless when there's nothing on them.

Then, like a sudden clap of thunder, it happened. It'd been so long since a spark of any kind, I barely held the pen as the words flowed, could hardly scribble fast enough to keep pace with my thoughts. I stopped writing before I was spent. I needed to hold the words like coins in my pocket to feed the meter, to fix the thing of the story in place until I came back to it the next day. Time existed again.

Then I slept. Not the fitful tortured sleep of the drying-out-drunk, but deep dream-filled sleep as if death had claimed me for the night but didn't quite know what to do with me.

After that, every day and most nights got easier. I don't know if I could have done it with him there or if his presence was part of my problem, as my at-no-cost-to-me therapist told me every Tuesday. My unresolved problems were fighting his unfinished business, like boxers who never landed the knockout punch, just bloodied and bruised waiting for someone to ring the bell or throw in the towel. It was all too complicated so I stopped listening to her and focused on memories of me and him, and our beautiful twisted history of love and forgiveness.

Occasionally my neighbor stood in as therapist number two and echoed the first. She would tell me over cups of hot coffee how he had contributed to my disease by always being there. I knew she was full of shit, but she meant well and she wasn't bad company while her husband was away. He'd gone to sea like mine, but for better reasons, or maybe worse. We were all working on something. I think she mostly liked the coffee. I knew she couldn't afford her own based on the day-old store-bought scones she would bring over, arrayed like crusty jewels atop a chipped floral piece of her better china.

James took the boat, sailing where he wanted while I figured out if I still wanted him, though I doubt he ever considered I might not be around when he came back. Thank God for miracles, minor and otherwise. The worst of winter came late. He made it to the sunshine states before he met his first storm.

Now autumn was upon us again, an early winter close on its heals. Our harbor town didn't have much to offer during the off season, all the regular boat taxis shut down, the docks clogged with the resident vessels waiting to be pulled from wet to dry, the big fishing boats doing what they always did, had always done, since there'd been a harbor clinging to the stony coast, fighting the waves, coming and going with the tide.

With the changing weather I offered to arrange his passage home, he could leave the boat in warmer water and fly back. He said no, that it wouldn't do either of us any good to change course. I believe it surprised him when I said I understood.

At the appointed hour, I stood on the shore waiting and watching, chilled by the wind over a sliver of white sand between the rolling granite of the New England coast.

It was and still is our secret place. The place we found by accident, though you'd think such a thing would have been found long before he or I ever walked this earth. I often wondered if the people in our ink-spot village had ceded it to us, as they had our private lives, no one interested in our love or torments for one another. Or perhaps it had been found before and each discoverer of the place made a sacred pact with the ocean to never give it away.

We spent hours on that tiny beach between the inland mountains and the rocks and cliffs of the coast. Dream-like hours, soft waves lulling us to sleep as the gulls peered down from the rocks and the sun kissed our flesh to bronze. Everything we had together was magical and horrible and bright and filled with shadows all at once.

He grew into his life and I curled like a drying leaf into mine, pulling away even as he held out hope each winter for an early spring. It took him years, but as he should have done, he left. His departing words were cast out like a lifeline to a drowning man, falling short by mere meters as the ship rolls by on the cresting waves driven by howling winds.

"I love you," he said, "but I can't live like this. Get yourself sorted, I'll be back in a year. You know where to meet me."

Of course I knew.

Cracks in the wet grey sky hinted at the promise of a last blue-sky day on the northern shore, held back as usual by the earth's slow spin and cantered angle to the sun. But the weather was no deterrent to my purpose.

I saw the mast first, thin as knife, slicing the air beyond the breakwater, white as the painted stone of the distant lighthouse guarding the bay. I kept my eye on it until the boat rounded the point. I watched from my distance as the sloop made gentle way into the waters we'd swum and paddled for years and considered the possibility it wasn't him. Strange to me how my vision faded then, a damp opacity, part of the game of getting older.

I spied a hand waving, not furtive, not exuberant, but waving all the same at me and no one else. Arrival took time, the usual steps of mooring, then the time of waiting for the water taxi rowboat to make its torturous way out to bring the yachtsman to shore, pulling against the waves and wind that skirted the breakwater. The old man at the oars knew James almost as well as I, a mentor of sorts to the young sailor. He seemed excited to go out against the cold and fetch him home to me.

The two men embraced, then spoke, exchanging words I could not hear. Whatever passed between them they smiled from it, that much I could see. James placed himself in the bow, looking at me across the open water as the oarsman plied his trade, the wind now behind him, the going easier, despite the added weight.

My heart raced when a gust of wind tossed his hair, now tinged grey-white against the dark black of his unkempt beard. He looked every bit the seasoned skipper, a presence I'd always chided him for failing to achieve in those years after he learned to sail. He leaned out over the bow and I allowed myself to imagine he was trying to reach me all the faster, propelling the skiff to shore by force of will.

When they arrived he sat back, the bow rose, and the boat slipped onto the beach with a gentle hush of wood against wet sand. He stepped out, his boots meeting the water, then turned to offer an assist to the oarsman, gliding him back off the beach, no words offered, exchanging never-ending smiles of two men who knew each other as they know the sea. They were friends, after all.

He turned back to me and to my surprise the smile did not vanish. Behind him the old man was making haste, but James' approach to me was slow, deliberate, paced in time to balance the rapid pounding of my heart, strong once again after years of abuse.

His beard fluttered at my face, teasing me with the promise of something more. He slipped his hand into mine, rough against my writer's palm, and leaned forward. I'd dreamed of the moment and thought then perhaps the moment was a dream. Then his kiss made it real. Soft and gentle, he conveyed all the passion of our years together in a silent moment with a delicate touch.

We held it long enough to know we didn't want it to end.

But the moment did end, as all moments do, and I was

rewarded once again with his smile. We stood a little longer, listening to the waves make love to the shore, steady rhythm of an ancient song, joined by the reed-like whistle of the wind.

I laced my fingers into his abundant beard. He leaned his head to the side, cradling himself in my palm, eyes closed as if asleep there in my hand. Time stopped for us then, in that intimate enclosure.

"How was it?" I asked.

"Farther than it looked," he replied, eyes still shut.

He opened his eyes and took my hand from his face and held it in his. His smile belied the hint of a tear growing below a hazel iris sparkling in defiance of the overcast sky.

"What now?" I asked, insecure even then.

"Home," he said, lifting the yolk of my suffering from my shoulders, "let's go home." Another smile, another gentle touch, one more kiss, then a soft rain began to fall, ushering us away from the water.

He slipped his arm around my waist, leaned against me, my own arm draped across his broad shoulders. We made our way up the road, wrapped in the warmth of our better memories. We tucked into our ancient cottage on the hill, looking down across the village and the bay, and set to the task of waiting out the winter, hoping as we did for an early spring and the return of the sun's seductive call.

He said he'd never leave again, and I accepted his word as truth.

We stayed there together until we each in our time found our end, ashes and dust to be spread across the water, becoming one with the wind and the sea and the shore, as we were meant to be, reunited at last with everything we'd ever loved.

An Understanding

The old man sat on his terrace listening to his ancient radio, his wheeled chair facing the ocean he could no longer see, obscured by new construction and failing vision. His beloved Key West, overgrown with people he'd never know, lived on only in his memories. He wore the clothes he chose by touch each morning before dawn, drawn from his over-large collection best described as vintage. He dressed from another time, as if waiting for a guest who would never come.

Isabella brought him his drink at the usual hour, a soda in a bottle, unopened. He struggled to twist off the cap, the bottle slippery from the condensation. "Let me," she said, reaching down, "don't you want a glass, with some ice?"

"No," he barked, and she stepped away, as she always did, then fell back into his orbit.

"Why do you treat me so? I have been here since before…"

"I'm near blind, woman, don't make it personal. Do you think I want this? Do you think I want to need you this way? Anyone can do this, you aren't special. Spare me your precocious feelings"

"You know my name," she said, and left him on the terrace to sort out his bottle of sugar and water. Until that day, she still saw the old man as he had been in better days, younger years, when the world beat a path to his door and begged for his genius, his artistry. When the years caught him and time took its toll, his partner, a man younger by decades, moved on to greener pastures. He was left alone and bitter to wonder where he'd gone wrong.

Only Isabella remained to nurture his rage, all the others faded away, found new heroes to worship. She remained trapped in her memories of the last good days, accepting his treatment of her as a burning badge of misplaced honor, love for a man incapable of returning her feelings.

The next day Isabella did not come to care for him. Someone different arrived, unannounced. She appeared long after the man who stayed with the old man through the night had left for the day. The night man's daily departure always left the old man sullen and grouchy, stirred up his memories of happier evenings devoid of longing and loneliness.

The old man was perplexed by the change he sensed, his agitation growing by leaps and bounds. He heard faint footsteps tapping through his entry hall. "Woman," he shouted, "I'm thirsty, the sun is beating me like a drum."

"I'm here," she whispered in his ear, startling him.

He drew the back of his hand across his forehead, scraping away the sweat. "Where's my drink?" he huffed.

"Beside you," she said, tracing the pointed nail of her index finger, a light touch of a sharp edge, along the dry parchment skin and coarse hair of his boney arm, "here on the table." Her hand reached his, she wrapped her delicate fingers around his wrist, lifted it, moving him toward the cool dripping glass of the bottle.

He snatched the bottle up toward his face, "Who are you?" he growled.

"I'm here, what does my name matter," she replied, her voice a cool breeze against the heat of the day.

He paused, began to speak, then took a sharp breath and spun off the cap. "You are not Isabella," he said.

"No," she replied, "I am someone new."

"New?" he laughed, "There's no such a thing as new. There's only the same old thing, bound in different cloth. There is nothing new."

His bitterness amused her. She smiled at the old man, ran her hand across his balding scalp, tickled one soft flapping ear lobe, then caressed a line along his scruffy chin. "You need a shave," she said, as if finding something hidden, "why hasn't the man looked after your face?"

"Hah," he choked out between swigs, "he's afraid to cut me. The woman is better, she looks after my beard."

"Old man," she said, her voice slipping into his ear, a gust of wind to fill a sail, "you have no beard, only a shadow on your chin. Shall I take care of it for you?"

"Fine, woman, if you must, but mind the scars, I don't need more."

She laughed in a way he knew was meant to tease him, so he allowed it as the shore allows the wave.

She left him for a while, then returned with the implements required for the task. She wrapped a towel around his neck, lathered his face, "Lean back" she said, and he did. She opened the blade, wiped it against the linen at her thigh, then dragged it across his cheek, beginning near his ear and swiping across his jawline.

A tiny bit of blood dribbled from an edge. She licked a bit of tissue and staunched the flow.

"You have a light touch," he said, "lighter than Isabella, but she never nicked me. Is this your first time?"

"Of course not," she answered, "now be still."

The old man did as he was told. He sat like a stone while she carved away, leaving his flesh fresh and new. When she finished, she wiped away the residue of her work, then stood to admire the results.

He ran a gnarled hand across his cheeks and chin, cracking

his rotten-tooth grin. "Smooth as a baby's bottom," he remarked, "you have the touch after all. What is your name?"

"Call me woman, if you like," she said, "or Marguerite."

He laughed at her then, he'd finally got the joke. "You're here to kill me I think," he said.

"No," she replied, "I'm here to set Isabella free."

"Then get it over with, I'm too old to waste time begging, you'll get none of it from me."

"Old man," she said, her laughter little birds flitting around a feeder, "your vanity…, it's too much."

She went inside, banging about his kitchen, leaving him there to feel the sun burning the pink flesh of his newly shaven face, too hot for the ocean breeze to cool. When she came back an hour later, his silent tears assured her the point had been made.

She draped a damp towel across his face, cold from the icebox. "Now old man," she whispered through his fear, "do we have an understanding?"

"Yes Marguerite," he said, flicking his tears away with a bony finger, voice muffled through the cooling towel, "we do."

She returned to the chattering screen door, then stopped when he said her name.

"Marguerite," he asked, his voice betraying his hope, "will Isabella be back tomorrow?"

"That is up to you old man," she said, then returned to the shaded interior of the stately crumbling home. The door banged shut, her footsteps echoed against the high ceiling and plaster walls. She began to sing a tune in time with his radio.

He sat in silence, his face no longer burning, the pounding of his heart slowed to a lesser beat. He listened to the woman sing, her voice dancing through the corridors and rooms of the house as she made her way back to the door, across the creaking boards, and down the stone steps, leaving him to wonder, for the first time in more years than he could remember, what the morrow might bring.

Lullaby

Old trains made noise, this much was certain. But this one, this one made music. The train lumbered along with its creaks, groans and rattles forming an unexpected rhythm that lulled its riders to sleep soon after it pulled away from their station.

Even the conductor barely stayed awake. He managed, long enough to collect the tickets, or sell them, as the case warranted. Now and again a traveller would board wide-eyed confused, a look he knew well, and he would pause long enough to explain where they were headed.

If they didn't like it, and protested just so, he would acquiesce and send them fluttering and flitting, back from whence they came. They'd be back soon enough, he knew, everyone always came back, some a little bit brighter. It was the nature of things, and he didn't mind, once in a while, bending the rules a bit.

It was their time, after all, until he took their ticket. Fine with him if they withered away some more before landing back aboard, listening to the old train's sweet ratchety lullaby, sleepily drifting onward toward the station they never reached.

It wasn't until they awoke they realized it was not the last, but only the next.

Then off they'd go, mingled souls and brightened spirits, each one among many now many become one, to explore and discover someplace new, filled with what they thought was wonder, 'til the next train came 'round to collect and carry them on again, to whatever waited down the line.

He loved his work, the conductor, especially that part about bending the rules. They were always happy, the ones he sent off, when they came back. That gift of extra time, of no meaning to him (just a flash, really), allowed occasion for things undone.

Some longed for completion in a fond farewell, old souls holding hands, time writ large in their wrinkled flesh, speaking volumes on sweet whispers as the day's light finally fades. For others, absolution. Forgiveness never sought and never offered, the parent and the child, 'til time closed the space between the two and truth, at last, could be told. Then there were the lovers who never loved, failing in their time to seize a precious moment, self-sabotaged by fear and inhibition, circling back to make a different choice, letting go a lifetime of regret.

However long they took, a day, a minute, years and years, it didn't matter. The conductor could always tell, when they handed over their ticket for the second time, how well they'd spent the nothing he had given them.

They'd climb the metal stairs, slip their hands along the burnished bronze, and slide across the darkened oak benches to stare through the crackle glass windows, waiting for the world to move.

The whistle would blow, the bell would clang-clang-clang, the wheels would turn, and the steam-stack billow out its great foamy cloud. The journey began, and the song played out once more.

This time though, they didn't mind the sleep.

About the Author

Ronald McGuire writes stories about change—how it arrives, how it reshapes us, and what remains in its wake. Blending literary and speculative elements, his fiction explores identity, memory, and the moments that define and redefine who we are.

He is the author of the novels *Beyond Tomorrow's Sun* and *Beyond the Rivers of Time*. *Nightmares & Lullabies* is his first collection of short fiction, to be followed by *Pax Liminalis in* August, 2026.

Ronald's work spans fiction, essays, journalism, and scriptwriting, with publication credits including Flash Fiction Magazine, Drunk Monkeys, The Dead Mule School of Southern Literature, Winning Writers, and CNN.com.

Learn more at ronaldmcguire.com or beachbookpress.com.